THE
BURNT
ORANGE
HERESY

THE
BURNT
ORANGE
HERESY

CHARLES WILLEFORD

THE OVERLOOK PRESS
NEW YORK, NY

Library of Congress Control Number: 2019938599

ISBN: 978-1-4197-5180-6
eISBN: 978-1-64700-189-6

Printed and bound in the U.S.A.
1 3 5 7 9 10 8 6 4 2

Abrams books are available at special discounts when purchased in quantity
for premiums and promotions as well as fundraising or educational use.
Special editions can also be created to specification. For details, contact
specialsales@abramsbooks.com or the address below.

ABRAMS The Art of Books
195 Broadway, New York, NY 10007
abramsbooks.com

For the late, great Jacques Debierue
c. 1886–1970
Memoria in aeterna

Nothing exists.
If anything exists, it is incomprehensible.
If anything was comprehensible,
it would be incommunicable.

—Gorgias

PART ONE

Nothing Exists

1

TWO HOURS AGO the Railway Expressman delivered the crated, newly published *International Encyclopedia of Fine Arts* to my Palm Beach apartment. I signed for the set, turned the thermostat of the air-conditioner up three degrees, found a clawhammer in the kitchen, and broke open the crate. Twenty-four beautiful buckram-bound volumes, eggshell paper, deckle edged. Six laborious years in preparation, more than twenty-five hundred illustrations—436 in full-color plates—and each thoroughly researched article written and signed by a noted authority in his specific field of art history.

Two articles were mine. And my name, James Figueras, was also referred to by other critics in three more articles. By quoting me, they gained authoritative support for their own opinions.

In my limited visionary world, the world of art criticism, where there are fewer than twenty-five men—and no women—earning their bread as full-time art critics (art reviewers for newspapers don't count), my name as an authority in this definitive encyclopedia means Success with an uppercase S. I thought about it for a moment. Only twenty-five full-time art critics in America, out of a population of more than two hundred million! This is a small number, indeed, of men who are able to look at art and understand it, and then interpret it in writing in such a way that those who care can share the aesthetic experience.

Clive Bell claimed that art was "significant form." I have no quarrel with that, but he never carried his thesis out to its obvious conclusion. It is the critic who makes the form(s) significant to the viewer! In seven more months I will reach my thirty-fifth birthday. I am the youngest authority with signed articles in the new Encyclopedia, and, I realized at that moment, if I lived long enough I had every opportunity of becoming the greatest art critic in America—and perhaps the world. With tenderness, I removed the heavy volumes from the crate and lined them up on my desk.

The complete set, if ordered by subscribers in advance of the announced publication date—and most universities, colleges, and larger public libraries would take advantage of the prepublication offer—sold for $350, plus shipping charges. After publication date, the *Encyclopedia* would sell for $500, with the option of buying an annual volume on the art of that year for only $10 (same good paper, same attractive binding).

It goes without saying, inasmuch as my field is contemporary art, that my name will appear in all of those yearbooks.

I had read the page proofs months before, of course, but I slowly reread my 1,600-word piece on art and the preschool child with the kind of satisfaction that any well-done professional job provides a reader. It was a tightly summarized condensation of my book, *Art and the Preschool Child,* which, in turn, was a rewritten revision of my Columbia Master's thesis. This book had launched me as an art critic, and, at the same time, the book was a failure. I say that the book was a failure because two colleges of education in two major universities adopted the book as a text for courses in child psychology, thereby indicating a failure on the part of the educators concerned to understand the thesis of the book, children, and psychology. Nevertheless, the book had enabled me to escape from the teaching of art history and had put me into full-time writing as an art critic.

Thomas Wyatt Russell, managing editor, *Fine Arts: The Americas,* who had read and understood the book, offered me a position on the magazine as a columnist and contributing editor, with a stipend of four hundred dollars a month. And *Fine Arts: The Americas,* which loses more than fifty thousand dollars a year for the foundation that supports it, is easily the most successful art magazine published in America—or anywhere else, for that matter. Admittedly, four hundred dollars a month is a niggardly sum, but my name on the masthead of this prestigious magazine was the wedge I needed at the time to sell freelance articles to other art magazines. My income from the latter source was uneven, of course, but with my assured monthly pittance it was enough—so long as I remained single, which was my avowed intention—to avoid teaching, which I despised, and enough to avoid the chilly confinement of museum work—the only other alternative open to those who selected art history as graduate degrees. There is always advertising, of course, but one does not deliberately devote one's time to the in-depth study of art history needed for a graduate degree to enter advertising, regardless of the money to be made in that field.

I closed the book, pushed it to one side, and then reached for Volume III. My fingers trembled—a little—as I lit a cigarette. I knew why I had lingered so long over the preschool child piece, even though I hated to admit it to myself. For a long time (I said to myself that I was only waiting to finish my cigarette first), I was physically unable to open the book to my article on Jacques Debierue. Every evil thing Dorian Gray did appeared on the face of his closeted portrait, but in my case, I wonder sometimes if there is a movie projector in a closet somewhere whirring away, showing the events of those two days of my life over and over. Evil, like everything else, should keep pace with the times, and I'm not a turn-of-the-century dilettante like Dorian Gray. I'm a professional, and as contemporary as the glaring Florida sun outside my window.

Despite the air-conditioning I perspired so heavily that my thick sideburns were matted and damp. Here, in this beautiful volume, was the bitter truth about myself at last. Did I owe my present reputation and success to Debierue, or did Debierue owe his success and reputation to me?

"Wherever you find ache," John Heywood wrote, "thou shalt not like him." The thought of Debierue made me ache all right—and I did not like the ache, nor did I like myself. But nothing, nothing in this world, could prevent me from reading my article on Jacques Debierue . . .

2

GLORIA BENTHAM DIDN'T know a damned thing about art, but that singularity did not prevent her from becoming a successful dealer and gallery owner in Palm Beach. To hold her own, and a little more, where there were thirty full-time galleries open during the "season," was more than a minor achievement, although the burgeoning art movement in recent years has made it possible to sell almost any artifact for some kind of sum. Nevertheless, it is more important for a dealer to understand people than it is to understand art. And Gloria, skinny, self-effacing, plain, had the patient ability to listen to people—a characteristic that often passes for understanding.

As I drove north toward Palm Beach on A1A from Miami, I thought about Gloria to avoid thinking about other things, but without much satisfaction. I had taken the longer, slower route instead of the Sunshine Parkway because I had wanted the extra hour or so it would take to sort out my thoughts about what I would write about Miami art, and to avoid, for an additional hour, the problem—if it was still a problem—of Berenice Hollis. Nothing is simple, and the reason I am a good critic is that I have learned the deep, dark secret of criticism. Thinking, the process of thinking, and the man thinking are all one and the same. And if this is true, and I live as though it is, then the man painting, the painting, and the process of painting are also one and the same. No one, and nothing, is ever simple, and Gloria had been anxious, too anxious, for me to get back to Palm Beach to attend the preview of her new show. The show was not important, nor was the idea unique. It was merely logical.

She was having a tandem showing of naive Haitian art and the work of a young Cleveland painter named Herb Westcott, who had spent a couple of months in Pétion-Ville, Haiti, painting the local scene. The contrast would make Westcott look bad, because he was a professional, and it would make the primitives look good, because they were naively unprofessional. She would sell the primitives for a 600 percent markup over what she paid for them and, although most of the buyers would bring them back after a week or so (not many people can live with Haitian primitives), she would still make a profit. And, for those collectors who could not stand naive art, Westcott's craftsmanship would look so superior to the Haitians' that he would undoubtedly sell a few more pictures in a tandem exhibit than he would in a one-man show without the advantage of the comparison.

By thinking about Gloria I had avoided, for a short while, thinking about Berenice Hollis. My solution to the problem of Berenice was one of mild overkill, and I half-hoped it had worked and half-hoped that it had not. She was a high school English teacher (eleventh grade) from Duluth, Minnesota, who had flown down to Palm Beach for a few weeks of sun-shiny convalescence after having a cyst removed from the base of her spine. Not a serious operation, but she had sick leave accumulated, and she took it. Her pale pink skin had turned gradually to saffron, and then to golden maple. The coccyx scar had changed from an angry red to gray and finally to slightly puckered grisaille.

Our romance had passed through similar shades and tints. I met Berenice at the Four Arts Gallery, where I was covering a traveling Toulouse-Lautrec exhibit, and she refused to go back to Duluth. That would have been all right with me (I could not, in all honesty, encourage anyone to return to Duluth), but I had made the mistake of letting her move in with me, a foolish decision that had seemed like a great idea at the time. She was a large—strapping is a better word—country girl with a ripe figure, cornflower-blue eyes, and a tangle of wheat-colored hair flowing down her back. Except for the thumb-tack scar on her coccyx, which was hardly noticeable, her sun-warmed sweet-smelling hide was flawless. Her blue eyes looked velvety, thanks to her contact lenses. But she wasn't really good natured, as I had thought at first, she was merely lazy. My efficiency apartment was too damned small for one person, let alone two, and she loomed in all directions. Seeing her dressed for the street or a party, no one would believe that Berenice was such a mess to live with—clothes strewn over every chair, wet bath towels, bikinis on the floor, the bathroom reeking of bath salts, powder, perfume, and unguents, a tangy mixture of smells so overpowering I had to hold my nose when I shaved. The state of the pullman kitchen was worse. She never washed cup, dish, pot, or pan, and once I caught her pouring bacon grease into the sink.

I could live with messiness. The major problem in having Berenice around all the time was that I had to do my writing in the apartment.

It had taken all of my persuasive abilities to talk Tom Russell into letting me cover the Gold Coast for the season. (The official "season" in Palm Beach begins on New Year's Eve with a dull dinner-dance at the Everglades Club, and it ends fuzzily on April 15.) When Tom agreed, finally, he refused to add expenses to my salary. I had to survive in Palm Beach on my monthly stipend, and pay my air fare down out of my small savings (the remainder of my savings bought me a

$250 car). By subletting my rent-controlled Village pad for almost twice as much as I was paying for it myself, I could get by. Barely.

I worked twice as hard, writing much better copy than I had in New York, to prove to Tom Russell that the Gold Coast was an incipient American art center that had been neglected far too long by serious art journals. Such was not truly the case, as yet, but there were scattered signs of progress. Most of the native painters of Florida were still dabbing out impressionistic palms and seascapes, but enough reputable painters from New York and Europe had discovered Florida for themselves, and the latter were exhibiting in galleries from Jupiter Beach to Miami. Enough painters, then, were exhibiting during the season to fill my *Notes* column on new shows, and at least one major artist exhibited long enough for me to honor him with one of my full-length treatments. There is money in Florida during the season, and artists will show anywhere there is enough money to purchase their work.

With Berenice around the tiny apartment all the time, I couldn't write. She would pad about barefooted, as quiet and as stealthy as a 140-pound mouse—until I complained. She would then sit quietly, placidly, not reading, not doing anything, except to stare lovingly at my back as I sat at my Hermes. I couldn't stand it.

"What are you thinking about, Berenice?"

"Nothing."

"Yes, you are, you're thinking about me."

"No, I'm not. Go ahead and write. I'm not bothering you."

But she did bother me, and I couldn't write. I couldn't hear her breathing, she was so quiet, but I would catch myself listening to see if I *could* hear her. It took some mental preparation (I am, basically, a kind sonofabitch), but I finally, in a nice way, asked Berenice to leave. She wouldn't go. Later I asked her to leave in a harsh and nasty way.

She wouldn't fight with me, but she wouldn't leave. On these occasions she wouldn't even talk back. She merely looked at me, earnestly, with her welkin eyes wide open—the lenses sliding around—tears torrenting, suppressing, or making an effort to hold back, big, blubbery, gasping sobs—she was destroying me. I would leave the apartment, forever, and come back a few hours later for a reconciliation replay and a wild hour in the sack.

But I wasn't getting my work done. Work is important to a man. Not even a Helen of Troy can compete with a Hermes. No matter how wonderful she is, a woman is only a woman, whereas 2,500 words is an article. In desperation I issued Berenice an ultimatum. I told her that I was leaving for Miami, and that when I came back twenty-four hours later I wanted her the hell out of my apartment and out of my life.

And now I was returning seventy-two hours later, having added two extra days as insurance. I expected her to be in the apartment. I wanted her to be there and, paradoxically, I wanted her to be gone forever.

I parked in the street, put the canvas top up on the Chevy—a seven-year-old convertible—and started across the flagged patio to the stuccoed outside staircase. Halfway up the stairs I could hear the phone ringing in my apartment on the second floor. I stopped and waited while it rang three more times. Berenice would be incapable of letting a phone ring four times without answering it, and I knew that she was gone. Before I got the door unlocked the ringing stopped.

Berenice was gone and the apartment was clean. It wasn't spotless, of course, but she had made a noble effort to put things in order. The dishes had been washed and put away and the linoleum floor had been mopped in a half-assed way.

There was a sealed envelope, with "James" scribbled on the outside, propped against my typewriter on the card table by the window.

Dearest dearest James—
You are a bastard but I think you know that.
I still love you but I will forget you—I hope I
never forget the good things. I'm going back
to Duluth—don't follow me there.
B.

If she didn't want me to follow her, why tell me where she was going?

There were three crumpled pieces of paper in the wastebasket. Rough drafts for the final note. I considered reading them, but changed my mind. I would let the final version stand. I crumpled the note and the envelope and added them to the wastebasket.

I felt a profound sense of loss, together with an unreasonable surge of anger. I could still smell Berenice in the apartment, and knew that her feminine compound of musk, sweat, perfume, pungent powder, lavender soap, bacon breath, Nose-cote, padded sachet coat hangers, vinegar, and everything else nice about her would linger on in the apartment forever. I felt sorry for myself and sorry for Berenice and, at the same time, a kind of bubbling elation that I was rid of her, even though I knew that I was going to miss her like crazy during the next few terrible weeks.

There was plenty of time before the preview at Gloria's Gallery. I removed my sport shirt, kicked off my loafers, and sat at the card table, which served as my desk, to go over my Miami notes. My three days in Dade County hadn't been wasted.

I had stayed with Larry Levine, in Coconut Grove. Larry was a printmaker I had known in New York, and his wife Paula was a superb cook. I would reimburse Larry with a brief comment about his new animal prints in my Notes column.

I had enough notes for a 2,500-word article on a "Southern

Gothic" environmental exhibit I had attended in North Miami, and an item on Harry Truman's glasses was a good lead-off piece for my back-of-the-book column. Larry had steered me to the latter.

A mechanic in South Miami, a Truman lover, had written to Lincoln Borglum, who had finished the monumental heads on Mount Rushmore after his father's death, and had asked the sculptor when he was going to add Harry Truman's head to the others. Lincoln Borglum, who apparently had a better sense of humor than his late father, Gutzon, claimed, in a facetious reply, that he was unable to do so because it was too difficult to duplicate Harry Truman's glasses. The mechanic, a man named Jack Wade, took Borglum at his word, and made the glasses himself.

They were enormous spectacles, more than twenty-five feet across, steel frames covered with thickly enameled ormolu. The lenses were fashioned from twindex windows, the kind with a vacuum to separate the two panes of glass.

"The vacuum inside will help keep the lenses from fogging up on cold days," Wade explained.

I had taken three black-and-white Polaroid snapshots of Wade and the glasses, and one of the photos was sharp enough to illustrate the item in my column. The spectacles were a superior job of craftsmanship, and I had suggested to Mr. Wade that he might sell them to an optician for advertising purposes. The suggestion made him angry.

"No, by God," he said adamantly. "These glasses were made for Mr. Truman, when his bust is finished on Mount Rushmore!"

The phone rang.

"Where have you been?" Gloria's voice asked shrilly. "I've been calling you all afternoon. Berenice said you left and that you might never come back."

"When did you talk to Berenice?"

"This morning, about ten thirty."

This news hit me hard. If I had returned in twenty-four hours, in forty-eight, or sixty—I'd still have Berenice. My timing had been perfect, but a pang was there.

"I've been in Miami, working. But Berenice has left and won't be back."

"Lovers' quarrel? Tell Gloria all about it."

"I don't want to talk about it, Gloria."

She laughed. "You're coming to the preview?"

"I told you I would. What's so important about second-hand Haitian art that you've had to call me all day?"

"Westcott's a good painter, James, he really is, you know. A first-rate draughtsman."

"Sure."

"You sound funny. Are you all right?"

"I'm fine. And I'll be there."

"That's what I wanted to talk to you about. Joseph Cassidy will be there, and he's coming because he wants to meet you. He told me so. You know who Mr. Cassidy is, don't you?"

"Doesn't everybody?"

"No, not everybody. Not everybody needs him!" She laughed. "But he's invited us—you and me and a few others—to supper at his place after the preview. He has a penthouse at the Royal Palm Towers."

"I know where he lives. Why does he want to meet me?"

"He didn't say. But he's the biggest collector to ever visit *my* little gallery, and if I could land him as a patron I wouldn't need any others—"

"Don't sell him any primitives, then, or Westcotts."

"Why not?"

"He isn't interested in conventional art. Don't try to sell him anything. Wait until I talk to him, and then I'll suggest something to you."

"I appreciate this, James."

"It's nothing."

"Are you bringing Berenice?"

"I don't want to *talk* about it, Gloria."

She was laughing as I racked the phone.

3

AS MUCH AS I dislike the term "freeloader," no other word fits what I had become during my sojourn on the Gold Coast. There are several seasonal societal levels in Palm Beach, and they are all quite different from the social groups, divided uneasily by the Waspish and Jewish groupings found in Miami and Miami Beach. In Lauderdale, of course, the monied class is squarely WASP.

I belonged to none of the "groups," but I was on the periphery of all of them by virtue of my calling. I met people at art show previews, where cocktails are usually served, and because I was young, single, and had an acceptable profession, I was frequently invited to dinners, cocktail parties, polo games, boat rides, late suppers, and barbecues. These invitations, which led to introductions to other guests, usually produced additional dinner invitations. And a few of the Gold Coast artists, like Larry Levine, for example, were people I had known in New York.

After two months in Florida I had many acquaintances, or connections, but no friends. I did not return any of the dinner invitations, and I had to avoid bars, night clubs, and restaurants where I might get stuck with a check. The man who never picks up a check does not acquire friends.

Nevertheless, I felt that my various hosts and hostesses were recompensed for my presence at their homes. I put up genially with bores, I was an extra man at dinners where single, heterosexual young men were at a premium, and when I was in a good mood, I could tell stories or carry conversation over dead spots.

I had two dinner jackets, a red silk brocade and a standard white linen. There were lipstick mouthings on the white jacket, where a tipsy Berenice had bitten me on the shoulder while I was driving back from a party. I was forced, then, to wear the red brocade.

As I walked the six blocks from my apartment to Gloria's Gallery, I speculated on Joseph Cassidy's invitation to supper. A social invitation wasn't unusual, but she had said that he wanted to meet me, and I wondered why. Cassidy was not only famous as a collector, he was famous as a criminal lawyer. It was the huge income from his practice in Chicago that had enabled him to build his art collection.

He had one of the finest private collections of contemporary art in America, and the conclusion I came to, which seemed reasonable at the time, was that he might want to hire me to write a catalogue for it. And if he did not want to see me about that (to my knowledge, no catalogue had been published on his collection), I had a good mind to suggest it to him. The task would pay off for me, as well as for Cassidy, in several ways. I could make some additional money, spend a few months in Chicago, do some writing on midwestern art and artists, and my name on the published catalogue would enhance my career.

The more I thought about the idea the more enthusiastic I became, but by the time I reached the gallery my enthusiasm was tempered by the knowledge that I could not broach the suggestion to him. If he suggested it, fine, but I could not ask a man for employment at a social affair without a loss of dignity.

And what else did I have to offer a man in Cassidy's position? My pride (call it *machismo*) in myself, which I overrated and which

I knew was often phony, was innate, I supposed—a part of my heritage from my Puerto Rican father. But the pride was there, all the same, and I had passed up many opportunities to push myself by considering first, inside my head, what my father would have done in similar circumstances.

By the time I reached the gallery, I had pushed the idea out of my mind.

Gloria forced her thin lips over her buck teeth, brushed my right sideburn with her mouth, and, capturing my right arm in a painful armlock, led me to the bar.

"Do you know this man, Eddy?" she said to the bartender.

"No," Eddy shook his head solemnly, "but his drink is familiar." He poured two ounces of Cutty Sark over two ice cubes and handed me the Dixie cup.

"Thanks, Eddy."

Eddy worked the day shift at Hiram's Hideaway in South Palm Beach, but he was a popular bartender and was hired by many hostesses during the season for parties at night. I usually ran into him once or twice a week at various places. Everybody, I thought, needs something extra nowadays. A regular job, and something else. Gloria, for example, wouldn't have been able to pay the high seasonal rent on her gallery if she didn't occasionally rent it out in the evenings for poetry readings and encounter-group therapy sessions. She detested these groups, too. The people who needed to listen to poetry, or tortured themselves in encounter-group sessions were all chain smokers, she claimed, who didn't use the ashtrays she provided.

Eddy worked at a sheet-covered card table. There was scotch, bourbon, gin and vermouth for martinis, and a plastic container of ice cubes behind the table. I moved back to give someone else a chance, and picked up a mimeographed catalogue from the table in the foyer.

Gloria was greeting newcomers at the door, bringing them to the table to sign her guest book, and then to the bar.

Her previews were not exclusive by any means. In addition to her regular guest list for previews, she gave invitations to Palm Beach hotel P.R. directors to hand out to guests who might be potential buyers. The square hotel guests, "honored" by being given printed preview invitations to a private show, and thrilled by the idea that they were seeing "real" Palm Beach society at an art show preview, occasionally purchased a painting. And when they did, the publicity director of the hotel they came from received a sports jacket or a new pair of Daks from Gloria. As a consequence, the preview crowd at Gloria's Gallery was often a weird group. There were even a couple of teenaged girls from Palm Beach Junior College peering anxiously at the primitives and writing notes with ballpoints in Blue Horse notebooks.

Herbert Westcott, I learned from the catalogue, was twenty-seven years old, a graduate of Western Reserve who had also studied at the Art Students League in New York. He had exhibited in Cleveland, the Art Students League, and Toronto, Canada. A Mr. Theodore L. Canavin of Philadelphia had collected some of his work. This exhibit, recent work done in Haiti during the past three months, was Westcott's first one-man show. I looked up from the catalogue and spotted the artist easily. He was short—about five seven—well tanned, with a skimpy, light brown beard. He wore a six-button, powder blue Palm Beach suit, white shoes, and a pale pink body shirt without a tie. He was eavesdropping on a middle-aged couple examining his largest painting—a Port-au-Prince market scene that was two-thirds lemon sky.

He drew well, as Gloria had said, but he had let his colors overlap by dripping to give the effect of fortuitous accident to his compositions. The drips—a messy heritage from Jackson Pollock—were injudicious. He had talent, of course, but talent is where a painter starts.

His Haitian men and women were in tints and shades of chocolate instead of black, something I might not have noticed if it had not been for the Haitian paintings on the opposite wall, where the figures were black indeed.

The dozen Haitian paintings Gloria had rounded up were all surprisingly good. She even had an early Marcel, circa 1900, so modestly different from the contemporary primitives with their bold reds and yellows, it riveted one's attention. The scene was typically Haitian, some thirty people engaged in voodoo rites, with a bored, comical goat as a central focusing point, but the picture was painted in gray, black, and white—no primary colors at all. Marcel, as I recalled, was an early primitive who had painted his canvases with chicken feathers because he could not afford brushes. It was priced at only fifteen hundred dollars, and someone would get a bargain if he purchased the Marcel . . .

"James," Gloria clutched my elbow, "I want you to meet Herb Westcott. Herb, this is Mr. Figueras."

"How do you do?" I said. "Gloria, where did you get the Marcel?"

"Later," she said. "Talk to Herb." She turned away, with her long freckled right arm outstretched to a tottering old man with rouged cheeks.

Westcott fingered his skimpy beard. "I'm sorry I didn't recognize you before, Mr. Figueras—Gloria told me you were coming—but I thought you wore a beard. . . ."

"It's the picture in my column. I should replace the photo, I suppose, but it's a good one and I haven't got another one yet. I had my beard for about a year before I shaved it. You shouldn't tug at your beard, Mr. Westcott . . ."

He dropped his hand quickly and shuffled his feet.

"I worked it all out, Mr. Westcott, and found that a beard would add about six weeks to my life, that is, six full weeks of shaving time saved in a lifetime, seven weeks if one uses an electric razor. But it wasn't worth it. Like you, I could hardly keep my fingers off the damned thing, and my neck itched all the time. The secret, they say, is never to touch your beard. And if you've already got that habit, Mr. Westcott, your beard is doomed."

"I see," he said shyly. "Thanks for the advice."

"Don't worry," I added, "you probably look handsomer without one."

"That's what Gloria said. Here," he took my empty Dixie cup—"let me get you a fresh drink. What are you drinking?"

"Eddy knows."

I turned back to examine the Marcel again. I wanted to leave. The small high-ceilinged room, which seemed smaller now as it began to get crowded, was jammed with loud-voiced people, and I did not want to talk to Westcott about his paintings. That's why I got off onto the beard gambit. They were all derivative, which he knew without my telling him. The entire show, including the Marcel, wasn't worth more than one column inch (I folded the catalogue and shoved it into my hip pocket), unless I got desperate for more filler to make the column come out to an even two thousand words.

Gloria was standing by the bar, together with a dozen other thirsty guests. Poor Westcott, who was paying for the liquor, hovered on the outskirts trying to get Eddy's attention. I took the opportunity to slip into the foyer and then out the door. I was on Worth Avenue in the late twilight, and heading for home. If Mr. Cassidy wanted to meet me, he could get my telephone number from Gloria and call for an appointment.

Twilight doesn't last very long in Florida. By the time I reached my ocherous predepression stucco apartment house—a mansion in the twenties, now cut up into small apartments—my depression was so bad I had a headache. I took off my jacket and sat on a concrete bench beneath a tamarisk tree in the patio and smoked a cigarette. The ocean wind was warm and soft. A few late birds twittered angrily as they tried to find roosting places in the crowded tree above my head. I was filled with emptiness up to my eyes, but not to the point of overflowing. Old Mrs. Weissberg, who lived in No. 2, was limping down the flagstone path toward my bench. To avoid talking to her I got up abruptly, climbed the stairs, heated a Patio Mexican Dinner for thirty minutes in the oven, ate half of it, and went to bed. I fell asleep at once and slept without dreams.

4

GLORIA SHOOK ME awake and switched on the lamp beside the Murphy bed. She had let herself in with the extra key I kept hidden in the potted geranium on the porch. She had either witnessed Berenice using the key or heard her mention that one was there. I blinked at Gloria in the sudden light, trying to pull myself together. My heart was still fluttering, but the burbling fear of being wakened in the dark was gradually going away.

"I'm sorry, James," Gloria said briskly, "but I knocked and you didn't answer. You really ought to get a doorbell, you know."

"Try phoning next time. I almost always get up to answer the phone, in case it might be something unimportant." I didn't try to conceal the irritation in my voice.

My cigarettes were in my trousers, which were hanging over the back of the straight chair by the coffee table. I slept nude, with just a sheet over me, but because I was angry as well as in need of a smoke, I threw the sheet off, got up and fumbled in the pockets of my trousers for my cigarettes. I lit one and tossed the match into the stoneware ashtray on the coffee table.

"This is important to me, James. Mr. Cassidy came and you weren't there. He asked about you and I told him you had a headache and left early—"

"True."

Gloria wasn't embarrassed by my nakedness, but now I felt self-conscious, standing bare assed in the center of the room, smoking and carrying on a moronic conversation. Gloria was in her late forties, and had been married for about six months to a hardware-store owner in Atlanta, so it wasn't her first time to see a man without any clothes on. Nevertheless, I took a terry-cloth robe out of the closet and slipped into it.

"He wants you to come to supper, James. And here I am, ready to take you."

"What time is it, anyway?"

"About ten forty." She squinted at the tiny hands on her platinum wristwatch. "Not quite ten forty-five."

I felt refreshed and wide-awake, although I had only slept two hours. Being awakened that way, so unexpectedly, had stirred up my adrenalin.

"I think you're overstating the case, Gloria. What, precisely, did Mr. Cassidy say to make you so positive he wanted me—in particular—to come to his little gathering?"

She rubbed her beaky nose with a skinny forefinger and frowned. "He said, 'I hope that Mr. Figueras' headache won't keep him from coming over this evening for a drink.' And I said, 'Oh, no. He asked me to pick him up later at his apartment. James is very anxious to meet you.' "

"I see. You turned a lukewarm chunk of small talk into a big deal. And now I have to go with you to get you off the hook."

"I wouldn't put it that way. He bought a picture from me, James, one of the primitives—the big one with the huge pile of different kinds of fruit. For his colored cook to hang in the kitchen."

"No Westcotts?"

"He didn't like Herb's pictures very well. I could tell, although he didn't say anything one way or another."

"I think he did. Buying a Haitian primitive for his cook says something, don't you think? Do I need another shave?"

She felt my chin with the tips of her fingers. "I don't think so. Brush your teeth, though. Your breath is simply awful."

"That's from the Mexican dinner I had earlier."

I dressed in gray slacks, a white shirt, and brown leather tie, dark brown loafers, and a gray-and-white striped seer-sucker jacket, resolving to take my soiled dinner jacket to the cleaner's in the morning. I remember how calm I was, and how well my mind seemed to be functioning after only two hours of sleep. All of my muscles were loose and stretchy. There was a spring to my step, as though I were wearing cushioned soles. I was in a pleasant mood, so much so that I pinched old Gloria through her girdle as we left the apartment.

"Oh, for God's sake, James!"

As we drove toward the Royal Palm Towers, a seven-story horror of poured concrete, in Gloria's white Pontiac, I found myself looking forward to meeting Mr. Cassidy and to seeing his paintings. He was bound to have a few pictures in his apartment, although his famous collection was safe in Chicago. I wondered, as well, why he had elected to live in the Royal Palm Towers, which overlooked Lake Worth instead of the Atlantic. He would be able to see the Atlantic from his rooftop patio, but only from a distance, and that wasn't the same as being on the beach.

The Towers was a formless mixture of rental apartments, condominium apartments, hotel rooms, and rental suites. The corporation that owned the building had overlooked very little in the way of income-producing cells. There were rental offices on the mezzanine (Cassidy also had a suite of offices there), and on the ground floor the corporation leased space for shops of all kinds, including a small art gallery. The coffee shop, the lounge-bar, and the dining room were all leased to various entrepreneurs. The corporation itself invested nothing in services and took from everybody. Cassidy probably maintained the penthouse, I decided, because the Royal Palm Towers was one of the few apartment hotels in Palm Beach that remained open all year round.

Many New Yorkers, who didn't like Florida for its climate, loved the state because there was no state income tax. By maintaining a residence for six months and one day in Florida they could beat New York's state income tax. An ignoble but practical motive for moving one's residence and business headquarters to Florida.

"Where," I asked Gloria, "did you get the Haitian primitives?"

"A widow in Lauderdale sold them to me." She giggled. "For a song. Her husband just died, and she sold everything—house, furniture, collection, and all. She was moving back to Indiana to live with her daughter and grandchildren."

"You priced the Marcel too low, baby. You can get more than fifteen hundred for it."

"I doubt it, and I can't lose anything—not when I only paid twenty-five dollars for it."

"You're a thief and a bitch."

Gloria giggled. "You're a blackguard. What have you done with Berenice?"

"She went back to Minnesota. I don't want to talk about her, Gloria."

"She's an awfully nice girl, James."

"I said I don't want to talk about her, Gloria."

We took the elevator to the penthouse, but the door didn't open automatically. There was a small one-way window on the steel door (a mirror on our side), and the Filipino houseboy checked us out before pressing the door release from his side. There was probably a release button concealed somewhere within the elevator cage. There had to be. Cassidy couldn't keep someone in his penthouse at all times, just to push a button and let him in—or could he? The very rich do a lot of strange things.

The party was not a large one. Seven people counting Mr. Cassidy. Gloria and I brought the total to nine. It was the kind of party where it is assumed that everyone knows one another and therefore no one is introduced. There are many parties like that in Palm Beach. The main idea is to eat first, and then drink as much as possible before the bar is closed or the liquor runs out. If one feels the need to talk to someone, he introduces himself or starts talking to someone without giving his name. It makes very little difference. Mr. Cassidy had to know everyone there—at least slightly—to brief the Filipino houseboy on the person's credentials for admittance.

Sloan, the bartender (he wore a name tag on his white jacket), poured us Cutty Sarks over ice cubes. I trailed Gloria toward the terrace, where Mr. Cassidy was talking to a grayhaired man who was probably a senior officer in some branch of the armed forces. He wore an Oxford gray suit with deeply pleated trousers. The suit was new, indicating that he didn't wear it often. This meant that he wore a uniform most of the time. A suit lasts army and navy officers for eight or nine years. Pleats were long out of fashion and Oxford gray is the favorite suit color for high-ranking officers. They lead dark, gray lives.

"I appreciate that, Tom," Cassidy said, sticking out his hand, and the gray-haired man was dismissed.

I watched the old-timer head for the elevator. I could have confirmed, easily enough, whether the man was in the service by asking, "Isn't that General Smith?" In this case, however, I believed that I was right and didn't feel the need of confirmation.

Joseph Cassidy was short, barely missing squatness, with wide meaty shoulders and a barrel chest. His tattersall vest was a size too small and looked incongruous with his red velvet smoking jacket.

He needed the vest for its pockets—pockets for his watch and chain, and the thin gold chain for his Phi Beta Kappa key. He had a tough Irish face, tiny blue eyes, with fully a sixteenth of an inch of white exposed beneath the irises, and square white teeth. His large upper front teeth overlapped, slightly, his full lower lip. His high forehead was flaking from sunburn. He wore a close-cropped black moustache, and his black hair, which was graying at the sides, was combed straight back and slicked down with water. Cassidy was a formidable man in his early fifties. He carried himself with an air of authority, and his confident manner was reinforced by his rich, resonant bass voice. And his gold-rimmed glasses—the same kind that Robert McNamara wore when he was Secretary of Defense—were beautifully suitable for his face.

Gloria introduced us and started toward the indoor fountain to look at the carp. The pool was crowded with these big fish, and I could see their backs, pied with gold and vermilion splotches, from where I stood, some fifteen feet away from the pool. A concrete griffin, on a pedestal in the center of the pool, dribbled water from its eagle beak into the carp-filled pool. It was a poorly designed griffin. The sculptor, who probably knew too much about anatomy, had been unable to come to terms with the idea of a cross between an eagle and a lion. Medieval sculptors, who knew nothing about anatomy, had no trouble at all in visualizing griffins and gargoyles. Cassidy took my arm, grasping my left elbow with a thumb and forefinger.

"Come on, Jim," he said, "I'll show you a couple of pictures. They call you 'Jim,' don't they?"

"No," I replied, hiding my irritation. "I prefer James. My father named me Jaime, but no one ever seemed to pronounce it right, so I changed it to James. Not legally," I added.

"It's the same name." He shrugged his meaty shoulders. "No need for a legal change, James."

I smiled. "I didn't ask for that advice, Mr. Cassidy, so please don't bill me for it."

"I don't intend to. I was just going to say that you don't look like a man named Jaime Figueras."

"Like the stereotype Puerto Rican, you mean? The peculiar thing is that my blond hair and blue eyes come from my father, not my mother. My mother was Scotch-Irish, with black hair and hazel eyes."

"You don't have a Spanish accent, either. How long have you lived in the States?"

"Since I was twelve. My father died, and my mother moved back to New York. She never liked Puerto Rico, anyway. She was a milliner, a creative designer of hats for women. You can't sell original hats to Puerto Rican women. All they need is a mantilla—or a piece of pink Kleenex pinned to their hair—to attend mass."

"I've never met a milliner."

"There aren't many left. My mother's dead now, and very few women wear originals nowadays, even when they happen to buy a hat."

"Are hats worth collecting?" he asked suddenly, moistening his upper lip with the tip of his pink tongue. "Original hats, I mean?"

I knew then that Mr. Cassidy was a true collector, and, knowing that, I knew a lot more about him than he thought I knew. In general, collectors can be divided into three categories.

First, the rare patron-collectors who know what they want and order it from artists and artisans. This first category, in the historical past, helped to establish styles. Without the huge demand for portraits in the sixteenth and seventeenth centuries, for example, there would have been no great school of portrait painters.

Second, the middle-ground people, who buy what is fashionable, but collect fashionable art because they either like it without knowing why (it reflects their times is why) or have been taught to like it.

In the third category are the collectors for economic reasons. They buy and sell to make a profit. That is, in a tautological sense, they are collectors because they are collectors, but they enjoy the works of art they possess at the moment for their present and future value.

The one trait that all three types of collectors have in common is miserliness. They write small, seldom dotting "i's" or crossing "t's" and they are frequently costive. Once they own something, *anything*, they don't want to give it up.

The collector's role is almost as important to world culture as the critic's. Without collectors there would be precious little art produced in this world, and without critics, collectors would wonder what to collect. Even those few collectors who are knowledgeable about art will not go out on a limb without critical confirmation. Collectors and critics live within this uneasy symbiotic relationship. And artists—the poor bastards—who are caught in the middle, would starve to death without us.

"No." I shook my head. As we crossed through the living room toward his study I explained why. "Hats are too easy to copy. Original hats, during the twenties and thirties, were expensive because they were made specifically for one person and for one occasion. As soon as a new hat was seen on Norma Shearer's head, it was copied and mass-produced. The copy, except perhaps for the materials, looked about the same. Some of the hats worn during the Gilded Age, when egret feathers were popular, might be worth collecting, but I doubt if restoration, storage, and upkeep costs would make it worthwhile to collect even those."

"I see. You have looked into it then?"

"Not exhaustively. Fashion isn't my field—as you know."

We entered his study, which was furnished in black leather, glass, and chrome. Cassidy sank into an audibly cushioned chair while I looked at the three pictures on the apple-green wall. There was an early Lichtenstein (a blown-up Dick Tracy panel), an airbrush Marilyn Monroe, in pale blue, from the Warhol series, and a black-and-white drawing of a girl's head by Matisse. The latter was over the ebony desk, in quiet isolation. The drawing was so bad Matisse must have signed it under duress. I sat across from Cassidy and put my empty glass on the rosewood coffee table. The Filipino house-boy appeared with a fresh drink on a tray, picked up my empty glass, and handed me the drink and a cocktail napkin.

"You wish something to eat, sir?"

"I think so. A turkey sandwich, all white meat, on white toast. With mayonnaise and cranberry sauce, and cut off the crusts, please."

He nodded and left.

"You don't like the drawing, do you?"

I shrugged, and sipped from my glass. "Matisse had a streak of meanness in him that many Americans associate with the French. When he went out to a café—after he became well known—he would often sketch on a pad, or sometimes on a napkin. Then, instead of paying his tab in cash, he'd leave the drawing on the table and walk out. The proprietor, knowing that the drawing was worth a good deal more than the dinner, was always delighted. A man full of rich food and a couple of bottles of wine doesn't always draw very well, Mr. Cassidy."

He nodded, relishing the story, and looked fondly at his Matisse. A bad drawing is a bad drawing, no matter who has drawn it. But my little story—and it was a true one—had merely enhanced the value of the Matisse for Cassidy. An ordinary person, if he had purchased a bad Matisse, would have felt gypped. But Cassidy wasn't an ordinary person. He was a collector, and not an ordinary collector.

"An interesting story." He smiled. "I don't have much here, and I haven't decided what to bring down from Chicago."

Here was a natural opening, and I took it. "I'd like to see the catalogue of your collection some time, Mr. Cassidy."

"Don't have one yet, but I've got a good man at the University of Chicago working on it. Dr. G. B. Lang. D'you know him?"

"Yes, but not personally. He wrote an excellent monograph on Rothko."

"That's Dr. Lang. It isn't costing me a dime, either—except for the printing costs. Dr. Lang teaches at the university, and one of my clients is on the Board of Trustees. Through him, my client, I managed to get Lang a reduced teaching schedule. He teaches two courses, and the rest of his load is research, the research being my catalogue. Dr. Lang's happy because he'll get another publication under his belt and, if he does a bang-up job, the University of Chicago Press will probably publish it."

When Cassidy smiled, exposing his teeth, his canines made little dents in his bottom lip. He stared at me for two long beats. His eyes, behind the gold-rimmed glasses, were flat and slightly magnified. He leaned forward slightly. "When men of good will get together, some sort of deal can be worked out to everyone's satisfaction. Isn't that right, James?"

"If they're 'men of good will,' yes. But my own experience has led me to believe that there aren't many of them around."

He laughed, as though I had said something funny. The house-boy brought my sandwich. I took a bite and called him back before he got out the door. "Just a minute! This isn't mayonnaise, this is salad dressing."

"Yes, sir."

"Don't you have any mayonnaise?"

"No, sir. May I bring you something else, sir?"

"Never mind."

In his own way, Joseph Cassidy was as famous as Lee Bailey. In court Cassidy was certainly as good a lawyer, but he wasn't as flamboyant with reporters outside of court as Bailey, nor did he take cases for sheer publicity value. He was a cash-in-advance, on-the-line lawyer. No one had written a biography on Cassidy yet, but he had socked away a lot more money than Bailey. His shrewdness in buying the right painters at the right time and at rock-bottom prices had made him another fortune—if he ever decided to put his collection on the market.

The houseboy still hovered about, wanting but unwilling to leave. He was upset because I didn't eat the sandwich.

"Close the bar, Rizal," Cassidy ordered quietly, "and tell Mrs. Bentham that I'll see that Mr. Figueras gets home all right." He exposed his toothy smile. "You don't mind sticking around for a while, do you, James?"

"Of course not, Mr. Cassidy."

Because of my upbringing, which has been on the formal side—insofar as observing the amenities was concerned—I resented the easy use of my first name by Mr. Cassidy without my permission or invitation. But I knew that he wasn't trying to patronize me. He was attempting to put me at my ease. Nevertheless, although I considered the idea, I couldn't drop to his level and call him Joe. There's too much informality in America as it is, and in Palm Beach, during the season, it is often carried to ridiculous lengths.

Rizal left to close the bar, which meant that the party was over. The guests would depart without saying good-bye to their host, and that would be that. Not out of rudeness, but out of deference. If Cassidy had gone out for a series of formal good-nights they would have adjusted to that kind of leave-taking just as easily.

After Rizal closed the door, Cassidy took a cigar out of his desk humidor, lighted it, and sat down again. He didn't offer me one.

"James," Cassidy said earnestly, "I know a lot more about you than you think I do. I rarely miss one of your critical articles, and I think you write about art with a good deal of insight and perception."

"Thank you."

"This is all straight talk, James. I'm not in the habit of handing out fulsome praise. A second-rate critic doesn't deserve it, and a first-rate critic doesn't need it. In my opinion, you're well on the way to becoming one of our best young American critics. And, according to my investigations, you're ambitious enough to be *the* best."

"By investigations, if you mean you've been talking to Gloria about me, she isn't the most reliable witness, you know. We've been friends for several years now, and she's prejudiced in my favor."

"No, not only Gloria, James, although I've talked to her, too. I've talked to dealers, to some of my fellow collectors, and even to Dr. Lang. You might be interested to know that Dr. Lang's highly impressed with your work, and he knows more about art history and criticism than I'll ever know."

"I'm not so sure about that, Mr. Cassidy."

"He should. That's his business—and yours. I'm an attorney, not an art historian. I don't even intend to write a foreword to my catalogue—although Lang suggested it to me."

"Most collectors do."

He nodded, and waved his right hand slowly so the ash wouldn't fall off the end of his cigar. "In the art world, you happen to have a reputation for integrity. And I've been informed that you're incorruptible."

"I'm not getting rich as an art critic, if that's what you mean."

"I know. I also know how to make inquiries. That's my business. The law is ninety-five percent preparation, and if a man does his homework, it's easy to look good in the courtroom. To return to corruption for a moment, let me say that I respect your so-called incorruptibility."

"The way you say it makes me feel as if I've missed some opportunity to make a pile of dough or something and turned it down. If I have missed out on something, I sure don't know about it."

"If you want to play dumb, I'll spell it out for you. Number one—free pictures. That kid's show this evening, ah, Westcott. Suppose you had said to Gloria that you would give Westcott a nice buildup in return for a couple of free pictures, what would have happened?"

"In Westcott's case, she'd have given *all* of them to me." I grinned. "But you aren't talking about integrity now, Mr. Cassidy, you're talking about my profession. I've never taken a free picture. The walls of my apartment in the Village are bare except for chance patterns of flaking paint. But if I ever took one picture, just one, that I could resell for two or three hundred bucks, the word would be out that I was on the take. From that moment on I would be dead as a critic. And a good review for pay, which is still being done in Paris, has damned near ruined serious art criticism in France.

"There are some exceptions, naturally, and those of us in the trade know who they are. So the way things are, I can't even afford to take legitimate art gifts from friends, even when I know that there are no strings attached. The strings would be there inadvertently. The mere fact that I took the gift might influence my opinion if I ever had to cover the man's show. By the same token, I don't buy anything either. And I've had some chances to buy some things that even I could afford. But if I owned a painting, you see, there might be a temptation on my part to push the artist beyond his worth—*possibly*—I don't know that I would—in order to increase the value of my own painting. I don't mean that I am completely objective either. That's impossible. I merely try to be most of the time, and that allows me to go overboard and be subjective as hell when I see something I really flip over."

I finished the last of my drink and set the glass down a little harder than I had intended. When I looked up, there was a smile on Cassidy's Irish face. Perhaps he had been baiting me, but I had been through this kind of probing before. It was natural, in America, for people to think that a critic had been paid off when he gave some artist a rave write-up, especially when they didn't know anything about art. But Cassidy knew better.

"You know all this, Mr. Cassidy, so don't give me any undeserved credit for integrity. I like money as much as anyone, and I made more money when I taught art history at CCNY than I do now. I'm ambitious, yes, but for a reputation, not for money. When I have a big enough reputation as a critic, then I'll make more money, but never a huge amount. That isn't the game. The trick—and it's a hard one—is to earn a living as an art critic, or, if you prefer, art expert. If you want me to authenticate a painting for you, I'll charge you a fee. Gladly. If you want to ask my advice on what to buy next for your collection, I'll give you suggestions free of charge." I held up my empty glass. "Except for another drink. Or is the bar closed for me, too?"

"I'll get the bottle." Cassidy left the room and returned almost immediately with an open bottle of Cutty Sark and a plastic bucket of cubes. I poured a double shot over two ice cubes and lit a cigarette. Cassidy picked up a yellow legal pad from his desk, sat down with it, and unscrewed the top from a fountain pen.

"I don't have any pictures for you to authenticate, James. And I didn't intend to ask you for any advice on collecting, but since you made the offer, what do you have in mind?"

I decided to tell him about my pet project.

"*Entartete Kunst.* Degenerate art."

"How do you spell that?"

I told him and he wrote it on the pad.

"It's a term that was used by Hitler's party to condemn modern art. At the time, Hitler was on an ethnic kick, and the official line was folk, or people's, art. Modern art, with its subjective individualistic viewpoint, was considered political and cultural anarchy, and Hitler ordered it suppressed. Even ruthlessly. Then, as now, no one was quite sure what modern art was, and it became necessary to make up a show of 'degenerate art' so that party men throughout Germany would know what in the hell they were supposed to prevent. So, in July 1937, they opened an exhibit of modern art in Munich. It was for adults only, so no children would be corrupted, and the exhibit was called *Entartete Kunst*. It was supposed to be an example, a warning to artists, and to people who might find such art attractive. After the Munich showing, it traveled all over Germany."

I leaned forward. "Listen to the names of the painters represented—Otto Dix, Emil Nolde, Franz Marc, Paul Klee, Kandinsky, Max Beckmann, and many more. I have a copy of the original catalogue in New York, locked away in the bottom drawer of my desk at the office."

"Those paintings would be worth a fortune today."

"The painters are all a part of art history now—and any of, say, Marc's paintings are expensive. But suppose you had every painting in this particular show? Every German museum was 'purified.' That was the term they used, 'purified.' And the painters represented by the show, if the museum happened to have any of their work, were removed. Some were destroyed, some were hidden, and some were smuggled out of the country. But to have the *original* traveling exhibit, and it would be *possible* to obtain these pictures . . ."

Cassidy drew a line through the two words on his pad and shook his head. "No, I could never swing anything like that by myself. I'd have to get a group together to raise the money, and—no, it wouldn't be worth it to me. Any more ideas?"

"Sure, but you didn't ask me here for my ideas on collecting."

"That's right. Basically, James, you and I are honest men, and, in our own ways, we are equally ambitious. One dishonest act doesn't make a person dishonest, not when it's the only one he ever performs. That is, a *slightly* dishonest act. A little thing, really. Suppose, James, that you were given the opportunity to interview"—he hesitated, moistened his lips with his tongue—"Jacques Debierue?"

"It would merely set me up with the greatest exclusive there is! But Debierue is in France, and he's only given three interviews in forty years—no, four—and none since his home burned down a year or so ago."

"In other words," he chuckled, "you would be somewhat elated if you could look at his new work and talk to him about it personally?"

"Elated isn't the word. *Ecstatic* isn't strong enough. Now that Duchamp is dead, Debierue is Mr. Grand Old Man of Modern Art."

"Don't go on, I know. Just listen. Suppose I told you that I could make arrangements for you to see and talk with Debierue?"

"I wouldn't believe you."

"But if it was true—and I am now telling you that it *is* true—what would you do for me in return?"

My throat and mouth were suddenly dry. I tipped the plastic ice bucket and poured some ice water into my empty glass. I sipped it, and it tasted almost warm. "You have something dishonest in mind. Isn't that what you implied a moment ago?"

"No. Not dishonest for you, dishonest for me. But even so, Debierue is in debt to me, if I want to look at it that way, and I do. I don't want money from him, I want one of his paintings."

I laughed. "Who doesn't? No individual, and not a single museum, has a Debierue. If you had one, you'd be the only collector in the world to have one! As far as I know, only four critics have been privileged to see any of his work. A servant or two has seen his paintings, probably, I don't know—maybe some of his mistresses a few years back, when he was still young enough to have them. But no one else—"

"I know. And I want one. In return for the interview, I want you to steal a picture for me."

I laughed. "And then, after I steal it, all I have to do is smuggle it back here from France. Right?"

"Wrong. And that's all I'll tell you now until I get a commitment from you. Yes or no. In return for the interview, you will steal a picture from Debierue and give it to me. No picture, no interview. Think about it."

"Hypothetically?"

"Not hypothetical. Actual."

"I'd do it. I *will* do it. That is, I'll steal one if he has any paintings to steal. Everything he had went up in smoke with his house, according to the reports. And if he hasn't painted anything since, well . . ."

"He has. I know that he has."

"You've got a deal. But I don't have the money for a round-trip air fare to France, not even for a slow freighter."

"Let's shake hands on it."

We got to our feet and shook hands solemnly. The palms of my hands were damp, and so were his, but we both gripped as hard as we could. He got the humidor and offered me a cigar. I shook my head and sat down. I started to pour another drink, but decided I didn't need it. My head was light and close to swimming. My heart was fluttering away as if I had swallowed a half-dozen dexies.

"Debierue," Cassidy laughed, a snort rather than an actual laugh, "is here in Florida, thirty-some-odd miles south, via State Road Seven. And that is my so-called dishonest act, my friend. I have just betrayed a client's confidence. A counselor isn't supposed to do that, you know. But now that I have, I'll tell you the rest of it.

"Arrangements were made for Debierue to come to Florida more than eight months ago, and I was the intermediary here. The emigration was set up by a Paris law firm, who contacted me, and I handled the matter on a no-fee basis, which I was glad to do. I rented the house—a one year lease—hired a black woman to come in and clean it for him once a week, bought his art supplies at Rex Art in Coral Gables, and picked him up at the airport. The whole thing. He's a poor man, as you know."

"And you're supporting him now?"

"No, no. The money comes from *Les Amis de Debierue*. You are—"

"I send them five bucks a year myself." I grimaced. "It's tax deductible, if I ever make enough money to list it among my many charities."

"Right. That's it. The Paris *Amis*, through the law firm, send me small sums more or less regularly, and I see that the old man's bills are paid—such as they are—and keep him in pocket money. He doesn't need much. The house is cheap, because of the rotten location. It was built by a man who retired to raise chickens. After six months of trying, and not knowing anything about poultry, he went back to Detroit. He's been trying to sell the house for two years, and was happy as hell to get a year's rent in advance." Cassidy smiled. "I even selected the old man's phony name for him—Eugene V. Debs. How do you like it?"

"Beautiful!"

"Better than beautiful. Debierue never heard of Gene Debs. And that's about it."

"Not quite. How did he get into the States without reporters finding out?"

"No problem. Paris to Madrid, Madrid to Puerto Rico, through the customs at San Juan, then on to Miami—and he came in on a student visa. J. Debierue. Who's going to suspect a man in his nineties on a student visa? And Debierue is a common enough name in France. There are about sixty flights a day from the Caribbean coming into Miami International on Sundays. It's the busiest airport in the world."

I nodded. "And the ugliest, too. So he's been right here in Florida for eight months?"

"Not exactly. The negotiations started eight months ago, and it took some time to set everything up. The funny thing is, the old man will actually be a student. I mentioned my connections at the University of Chicago—well, starting in September, Debierue will be taking twelve hours of college credit, by correspondence, from Chicago."

"What's his major?"

"Cost accounting and management. I've got a young man working for me who can whip through those correspondence courses with his left hand, and he'll probably get the old man an A average. On a student visa, you see, you have to carry twelve hours a semester to stay in the country. As long as you're making good grades with the college, you can stay as long as you like."

"I know. But why me? Why don't *you* steal a picture from Debierue?"

"He'd know it was me, that's why. After I got him settled, he told me he didn't want me to visit him. For the sake of secrecy. I went down a couple of times anyway and pestered him for a painting. He got good and angry the last time, and his studio is kept padlocked. I want one of his paintings. I don't care what it is, or whether anyone knows that I have one. *I'll* know, and that's enough. For now. Of course, if you manage to get a successful interview—and that's your problem—and you write about his new work—he hasn't got *too* many years to live—then I can bring my painting out and show it. Can't I?"

"I understand. You'll have pulled off the collector's coup of this decade—but what happens to me?"

"You'll stand still for it, no matter what happens. I've checked you out, I told you. You're ambitious, and you'll be the first, as well as the *only*, American critic to have an exclusive interview with the great Jacques Debierue. After you steal one of his pictures, he sure as hell won't talk to anyone else."

"What time is it set up for, and when?"

"It isn't. That's up to you." He wrote the address on the yellow pad, and sketched in State Road Seven and the branch road leading into it from Boynton Beach. "If you happen to drive past the turnoff, and you might miss Debierue's road because it's dirt and you can't see the house from the highway, you'll know you missed it when you spot the drive-in movie about a half mile farther on. Turn around and go back."

"Does he know I'm coming?"

"No. That's your problem?"

"Why did he decide to come to Florida?"

"Ask him. You're the writer."

"He might slam the door in my face, then?"

"Who knows. We made a deal, that's all, and we shook hands on it. I know my business, and you should know yours. Any more questions?"

"Not for you."

"Good." He got to his feet, an abrupt signal that the discussion was finished. "When are you driving down?"

"That's my business." I grinned, and stuck out my hand.

We shook hands again, and Cassidy asked kindly if he could telephone for a taxi. Sending me home in a cab at my own expense was his method of "seeing that I got home all right."

I declined, and rode down in the elevator. To clear my head, I preferred to walk the few blocks to my apartment. As I walked the quiet streets through the warm soft night, a Palm Beach police car, staying a discreet block behind, trailed me home. I wasn't suspected of anything. The cops were merely making certain that I would get home all right. Palm Beach is probably, together with Hobe Sound, the best-protected city in the United States.

Now that I was alone, I was so filled with excitement I could hardly think straight. Dada, first, and Surrealism, second, were my favorite periods in art history. And because of my interest in these movements when I had been in Paris, I knew the Paris art scene of the twenties better, in many respects, than most of the people who had participated in it. And Debierue—Jacques Debierue! Debierue was the key figure, the symbol of the dividing line, if a line could be delineated, in the split between Dada and Surrealism! In my exhilarated state, I knew I wouldn't be able to sleep. I was going to put on a pot of coffee and jot down notes on Debierue from memory in preparation for the interview. Tomorrow, I thought, *tomorrow!*

I turned the key in the door and opened it to unexpected light. The soft light streamed in from the bathroom. Silhouetted in the bathroom doorway, wearing a gray-blue shorty nightgown, was my tawny-maned schoolteacher. Her long, swordlike legs trembled at the knees.

"I—I came back, James," Berenice said tearfully.

I nodded, dumbly, and lifted my arms so she could rush into them. After she calms down, I thought, I'll have her make the coffee. Berenice makes much better coffee than I do . . .

5

DEBIERUE IS A difficult artist to explain, I explained to Berenice over coffee:

"*No pido nunca a nadie* is a good summary of the code Debierue's lived by all his life. Translated, it means, 'I never ask nobody for nothing.'"

"I think that's the first time I've ever heard you talk in Spanish, James."

"And it might be the last. It didn't take me long to quit speaking Spanish after we moved to New York from San Juan. And as soon as I wised up to how they felt about Puerto Ricans, I got rid of my Spanish accent, too. But the Spanish *No pido nunca a nadie* sounds better because the reiterated double negatives don't cancel each other out as they do in English. And that's the story of Debierue's life, one double negative action after another until, by not trying to impress anybody, he ended up by impressing everybody."

"But why did you give up speaking Spanish?"

"To prove to myself, I suppose, that a Puerto Rican's not only as good as anybody else, he's a damned sight better. Besides, that's what my father would've done."

"But your father's dead, you told me—"

"That's right. He died when I was twelve, but technically I never had a father. He and my mother separated before I was a year old, you see. They didn't get divorced because they were Catholics, although my mother made semi-official arrangements with the church for them to live apart. There was no money problem. He supported us until he died, and then we came up to New York, Mother and I, with the insurance and the money from the sale of our house in San Juan."

"But you saw him once in a while, didn't you?"

"No. Never. Not after their separation—except in photographs, of course. That's what made things so tough for me, Berenice. What I've had instead is an imaginary father, a father I've had to make up myself, and he's what you might call *un hombre duro*—a hard man."

"What you mean, James, you've deliberately made things hard on yourself."

"It isn't that simple. A boy who doesn't have a father around doesn't develop a superego, and if you don't get a superego naturally you've got to invent one—"

"That's silly. Superego is only a jargon word for 'conscience,' and everybody's got a conscience."

"Have it your way, Berenice, although Fromm and Rollo May wouldn't agree with you."

"But *you've* got a conscience."

"Right. At least I've got one intellectually, if not emotionally, because I was smart enough to create an imaginary father."

"Sometimes I don't understand you, James."

"That's because you're like the little old lady in Hemingway's *Death in the Afternoon*."

"I've never read it. That's his book on bullfighting, isn't it?"

"No. It's a book about Hemingway. By talking about bullfighting he tells us about himself. You can learn a lot about bullfighting in

Death in the Afternoon, but what you learn about life and death is a matter of Hemingway."

"And the little old lady . . . ?"

"The little old lady in *Death in the Afternoon* kept asking irrelevant questions. As a consequence, she didn't learn much about bullfighting or Ernest Hemingway and toward the end of the book Hemingway has to get rid of her."

"I'm not a little old lady. I'm a young woman and I can learn. And if I want to understand you better, I should listen to what you have to say about art because it's a matter of life and death to you."

"You might put it that way."

"I am putting it that way."

"Would you like to hear about Jacques Debierue?"

"I'd love to hear about Jacques Debierue!"

"In that case, I'll begin without the overall frame of reference and fill in the necessary background as I come to it. I said, I'll begin without the—I see, you don't have any relevant questions and you've decided to remain silent until you do? Fine. You'll understand my exhilaration about my opportunity to meet Jacques Debierue, then, when I tell you that I've read all, as far as I know, that's been written about him. The scope is wide, but the viewpoint is narrow.

"Only four other critics, all Europeans, have actually seen and written about his work at firsthand. I'll be the first American critic to examine his work, and it'll be new, original painting that no one else has ever seen before. For the first time in my critical career, I'll see the most recent Nihilistic Surrealistic paintings by the most famous artist in the world. It will also be possible, afterward, for me to evaluate and compare my opinions with the critiques of those critics who've written about his earlier work. I'll have a broad view of Debierue's growth—or possible retrogression—and historical support, or better yet, nonsupport, for my convictions.

"The incidental factors that led to Debierue's fame during the course of contemporary art history are marvelous. His silent, uphill fight against improbable odds appears, on the surface, to be effortless, but such was not the case. Mass hostility is always omnipresent toward the new, especially in art. Hundreds of books, as you know, have been filled with exegetical opinions about the Impressionists, Expressionists, Suprematists, Cubists, Futurists, Dadaists, and Surrealists of the early years of this century. All of the major innovators have been examined in detail, but there were many other painters who received no recognition at all. And there were smaller movements that were formed and then dissolved without being mentioned. How many, no one knows.

"But it was these minor movements that I was interested in during my year in Europe. It was a way to earn a reputation, you see. And if I could've pinned *one* of them down, one that got away, a movement that I could've written about and established as an important but overlooked movement in art history, I could've started my critical career immediately instead of teaching art survey courses to bored accountants at CCNY.

"Paris seethed with new developments in art before, during, and after the First World War. Hardly a day passed without a new group being formed, a new manifesto being drafted, followed by polemics, fistfights, dissolvements.

"Three painters would meet in a café, argue affably among themselves until midnight, and decide to form their own little splinter group. Then, as wine and arguments flowed for the remainder of the night as they scribbled away at a new manifesto, they detested each other by dawn.

"White-faced with anger and lack of sleep, they'd march off to their studios in the nacreous light of morning, their new movement junked before it was begun.

"A few of these lesser movements caught on, however, lasting for a few days or weeks after a scattered flurry of press publicity, but most of them died unheralded, unnoticed, for want of a second—or for no discernible reason. The fortunate, well-publicized movements lasted long enough to influence enough imitators to gain solid niches in art history. Cubism, for example, a term that pleased the reading public, was one of them.

"Paris, of course, was the center of the vortex during the early twenties, but forays into new and exciting art expressions were by no means confined to France.

"During my single year in France, as I tried to track down tangible evidence of these minor movements without success, my side trips to Brussels and Germany were even more tantalizing.

"In Brussels, the Grimm Brothers, Hal and Hans, who called themselves 'The Grimmists,' spent months in dark mines collecting expressive lumps of coal. These were exhibited as 'natural' sculptures on white satin pillows. Within two days, however, shivering Belgians had pilfered these exposed lumps of coal, and the exhibit closed. The Belgians are a practical people, and 1919 was a cold winter. In their own way, the Brothers Grimm had originated 'Found' art—"

"James—when you say that you have no superego, or conscience, does that mean that you've never done anything *bad*, anything you've ever been sorry for, later?"

"Yeah. Once. There was an assistant professor I knew at Columbia, an anthropologist, whose wife died. He had her cremated, and bought a beautiful five-hundred-dollar urn to keep her ashes in. He used to keep the urn on his desk at home, as a *memento mori*. Anthropologists, as you know, are pretty keen on ritual, burial ceremonies, and pottery—things of that nature. His wife died of tuberculosis.

"I never knew his first wife, but I met his second wife, who was one of his graduate students. Men, like women, are usually attracted to the same type of person when they remarry—"

"That isn't true! I've never known anyone like you before—"

"But then you've never been married, Berenice. And I'm talking about a widower who married again. His name doesn't matter to you, but it happened to be Dr. Hank Goldhagen. Anyway, his second wife, Claire, was *also* susceptible to respiratory infections. Sometimes, when they got into an argument, Hank would point to the urn of ashes, and say, 'My first wife, in that urn, is a better woman and a better wife to me than you are, right now!' "

"What a terrible thing to say!"

"Isn't it? I sometimes wonder what she said to him to provoke it. But the marriage didn't last long. Following a weekend skiing trip to New Hampshire, Claire developed lumbar pneumonia and died. To save Hank money, I advised him to put Claire's ashes in the same expensive urn with his first wife."

"But why . . . ?"

"There was ample room in the urn, and why not? Did it make any sense to buy a second expensive urn? And if he bought a cheaper one, that would've indicated to his friends that he thought less of Claire than he did of his first wife. But my practical suggestion backfired. Hank got so he was staring at the urn all the time brooding over and about the mixed ashes of these two women, and eventually he cracked up. And because it was my fault, I felt bad about it for weeks."

"That isn't a true story, is it? Is it, James?"

"No, it isn't a true story. I made it up to please you, because, it seems, you're a little old lady who likes stories."

"No, I'm not—and I don't like stories like that!"

"I'm leading up to Debierue, and I promise you that it's much more interesting than the story of Dr. Goldhagen's two wives."

"I'm sorry I interrupted, James. May I pour you another cup of coffee?"

"Please. Let me tell you first about the *Scatölögieschul* that was formed by Willy Büttner in Berlin, during the post-war years of German political art. The *Scatölögieschul* probably holds the European record for short-livedness. It opened and closed in eight minutes flat. Herr Büttner and his three defiant fellow exhibitors, together with their cretin model—who denied her obvious presence in every painting—were carted off to jail. The paintings were confiscated, never to be seen by the public again. According to rumor, these ostensibly pornographic paintings wound up in General Goering's private collection. They're now believed to be in Russia, but no one really knows. I couldn't find a single eyewitness who had seen the pictures, although a lot of people knew about the exhibit. This was another frustrating experience for me in Europe.

"By the early sixties the trail was too cold for valid, documentary evidence. I was too late. The European Depression and World War Two had destroyed the evidence. I still feel that the critical neglect of these so-called minor movements may prove to be an incalculable loss to art history. Then, as now, critics only choose a very small number of painters to be *the* representatives of their times. And we only remember the names of those who come in first. Any sports writer can recall that Jesse Owens was the fastest runner in the 1936 Olympics, but he won't remember the names of the second and third place runners who were only split seconds behind him.

"Therefore, it's almost miraculous that Jacques Debierue was noticed at all. When you think about the peculiar mixture of hope and disillusionment of the twenties, he seems to be the most unlikely candidate of all the artists of the time to be singled out for fame. And he was studiedly indifferent to the press.

"One painter, a true archetype, can hardly be said to constitute a movement, but Debierue rose above the Parisian art world like an extended middle finger. Paris critics found it embarrassing to admit that none of them knew the exact date his one-man show opened.

The known details of the discovery of Debierue, and the impact of his influence on other painters, has been examined at some length by August Hauptmann in his monograph entitled *Debierue*. This isn't a long book, not for the work of a German scholar, but it's a well-documented study of Debierue's original achievement.

"There isn't any mass of published work on Debierue, as there is on Pablo Picasso, but Debierue's name crops up all the time in the biographies and autobiographies of other famous modern painters—usually in strange circumstances. The frequent mention of his name isn't surprising. Before Debierue was in the art world, he was of it. Because he framed their paintings, he knew personally, and well, most of the other firsts of the war and postwar years."

"He was a picture framer?"

"At first, yes. Miró, De Chirico, Man Ray, Pierre Roy, and many other painters found it expedient to visit him in his tiny framing shop. He gave them credit, and until they started to make money with their work, they sorely needed credit. Debierue's name is brought up in the studies published on every important postwar development because he was there—and because he knew all the artists involved. But his only commonality with other innovators is the fact that he was a first in his own right as the acknowledged father of Nihilistic Surrealism. Debierue, by the way, didn't coin this term for his work.

"The Swiss essayist and art critic, Franz Moricand, was the first writer to use this term with reference to Debierue's art. And the label, once attached, stuck. The term appeared originally in Moricand's essay, "*Stellt er nur?*" in *Mercure de France*. The article wasn't penetrating, but other critics were quick to snatch the term 'Nihilistic Surrealism' from the essay. An apt and descriptive bridge was needed, you see, to provide a clear dividing line between Dada and Surrealism. Both groups have attempted at various times to claim Debierue, but he was never in either camp. Dada and Surrealism both have strong philosophical underpinnings, but no one knows what Debierue's leanings are.

"Chance is an important factor in the discovery and recognition of every artist, but what many modern critics fail to accept is that Debierue's many artist-friends paid off by sending people to see Debierue's one-man show. In his Montmartre hole-in-the-wall framing workshop he had mounted many paintings at cost, and others absolutely free, for poor young painters whose work sold a few months later for high prices. Those 'crazy boatloads' of Americans, as Fitzgerald called them, coming to France during the boom period, always carried more than fifty dollars in cash on their person. They bought a lot of paintings, and the selling painters didn't forget their obligations to Debierue.

"Despite Hauptmann's book, an aura of mystery about Debierue's first and only one-man show remains. No invitations were issued, and there were no posters or newspaper ads. He didn't even mention the show to his friends. One day, and the exact date is still unknown, a small, hand-lettered card appeared in the display case behind the street window of his framing shop. 'Jacques Debierue. *No. One.* Shown by request only.' It was spelled Capital N-o-period. Capital O-n-e."

"Why didn't he use the French *Nombre une?*"

"That's a good point, Berenice. But no one really knows. The fact that he used the English *No. One* instead of *Nombre une* may or may not've influenced Samuel Beckett to write in French instead of English, as the literary critic Leon Mindlin has claimed. But everyone concerned agrees that it was an astute move on Debierue's part when American tourists, with their limited French, began to arrive on the Paris scene. Using a number as a title for his picture, incidentally, was another first in art that has been indisputably credited to Debierue. Rothko, who uses numbers exclusively for his paintings, has admitted privately, if not in writing, his indebtedness to Debierue. The point's important because several art historians falsely attribute the numbering of paintings as a first for Rothko. Debierue hasn't said anything, one way or another, about the matter. He's never commented on his picture, either.

"This much is certain. *No. One* postdated Dada and predated Surrealism, thereby providing a one-man bridge between the two major art movements of this century. And Debierue's Nihilistic Surrealism may, in time, turn out to be the most important movement of the three. In retrospect, it's easy enough for us to see how Debierue captured the hearts and minds of the remaining Dadaists who were gradually, one by one, dropping out of Dada and losing their hard-earned recognition to the burgeoning Surrealists. And you can also realize, now, why the Surrealists were so anxious to claim Debierue. But Debierue stood alone. He neither admitted nor denied membership in either movement. His work spoke for him, as a work of art is supposed to do.

"*No. One* was exhibited in a small and otherwise empty room— once a maid's bedroom—one short flight of stairs above Debierue's downstairs workshop. An environment had been created deliberately for the picture. The visitor who requested to see it—no fee was asked—was escorted upstairs by the artist himself and left alone with the picture.

"At first, as the viewer's eyes became adjusted to the murky natural light coming into the room from a single dirty window high on the opposite wall, all he could see was what appeared to be an ornate frame, without a picture in it, hanging on the wall. A closer inspection, with the aid of a match or cigarette lighter, revealed that the gilded frame with baroque scrollwork enclosed a fissure or crack in the gray plaster wall. The exposed wire, and the nail which had been driven into the wall to hold both the wire and the frame, were also visible. Within the frame, the wire, peaking to about twenty degrees at the apex—at the nail—resembled, if the viewer stood well back from the picture, a distant mountain range."

Berenice sighed. "I don't understand it. The whole thing doesn't make any sense to me."

"Exactly! No sense, but not nonsense. This was an irrational work in a rational setting. Debierue's Nihilistic Surrealism, like Dada and Surrealism, is irrational. That's the entire point of Dada, and of most of the other postwar art movements. Distortion, irrationality, and the unlikely juxtaposition of objects."

"What did the reviewers say about it?"

"What the reviewers said in the newspapers isn't important, Berenice. There's a distinction between a reviewer and a critic, as you should know. The reviewer deals with art as a commodity. He's got three or four shows a week to cover, and his treatment of them is superficial, at best. But the critic is interested in aesthetics, and in placing the work of art in the scheme of things—or even as a pattern of behavior."

"All right, then. What did the critics say about *No. One?*" "A great many things. But criticism begins with the structure, and often ends there, especially for those critics who believe that every work of art is autotelic. Autotelic. That means—"

"I know what autotelic means. I studied literary criticism in college, and I've got a degree in English."

"Okay. What does it mean?"

"It means that a work of art is complete in itself."

"Right! And what else does it mean, or imply?"

"Just that. That the poem, or whatever, should be considered by itself, without reference to anything else."

"That's right, but there's more. It means that the artist himself should not be brought into the criticism of the work being considered. And although I'm a structuralist, I don't think that any work—poem, painting, novel—is autotelic. The personality of the artist is present in every work of art, and the critic has to dig it out as well as explicating the structure and form. Take pro football—"

"I'd love to. It's more interesting than painting."

"To you, yes, but I want to make an analogy. A good critic's like a good football announcer on television. We see the same play that he does, but he breaks it down for us, reveals the structure and the pattern of the play. He explains what went wrong and what was right about the play. He can also tell us what is likely to come next. Also, because of the instant tape replay, he can even break down the play into its component parts for us to see again in slow motion. We do the same thing in art criticism sometimes, when we blow up details of a painting in slides."

"Your analogy doesn't explain the 'personality' in the football play."

"Yes it does. This is the quarterback, who caused the play in the first place. That is, if the quarterback called the play. Sometimes the coach calls every play, sending in the new play every time with a substitute. If the announcer doesn't know what the coach is like, what he has done before, *or* the quarterback, I'll say, his explanation of the structure of the play is going to be shaky, and any prediction he makes won't be valid. Do you follow me?"

"I follow you."

"Good. Then you shouldn't have any trouble in understanding the success of *No. One*. Only one person at a time was allowed to examine the picture. But there was no time limit set by the artist. Some visitors came downstairs immediately. Others remained for an hour or more, inconveniencing those waiting below. The average viewer was satisfied by a cursory inspection. But according to Hauptmann, there were a great many repeats.

"One old Spanish nobleman from Sevilla visited Paris a half-dozen times for the sole purpose of taking another look at *No. One*. No visitor's log was kept, but the fact that a vast number of people visited Debierue's shop to see the picture is a matter of public record. Every Parisian artist of the time made the pilgrimage, usually bringing along some friends. And *No. One* was widely discussed.

"Sporadic newspaper publicity, the critical attention Debierue provoked in European art reviews, and word-of-mouth discussion of the exhibit, brought a steady stream of visitors to his gallery until May 25, 1925, when he sold his shop for the purpose of painting full time.

"*No. One,* naturally, was a picture that lent itself to varied, conflicting opinions. The crack enclosed by the mount, for example, might've been on the wall before Debierue hung the frame over it—or else it was made on purpose by the artist. This was a basic, if subjective, decision each critic had to make for himself. The conclusions on this primary premise opened up two diametrically opposed lines of interpretive commentary. The explicit versus the implicit meaning caused angry fluctuations in the press. To hold any opinion meant that one had to see the picture for himself. And the tiny gallery became a 'must see' for visiting foreign journalists and art scholars.

"Most of the commentators concentrated their remarks on the jagged crack within the frame. But there were a few who considered this point immaterial because the crack couldn't be moved if the frame were to be removed. They were wrong. A critic has to discuss what's there, not something that may be somewhere else. And he never exhibited it anywhere else after he sold his shop. The consensus, including the opinions of those who actually detested the picture, was an agreement that the crack represented the final and inevitable break between traditional academic art and the new art of the twentieth century. In other words, *No. One* ushered in what Harold Rosenberg has since called 'the tradition of the new.'

"Freudian interpretations were popular, with the usual sexual connotations, but the sharpest splits were between the Dadaists and the Surrealists concerning the irrational aspects of the picture. Most Surrealists (Buñuel was an exception) held the opinion that Debierue had gone too far, feeling that he had reached a point of no return. Dadaists, many of them angered over the use of a gilded baroque mounting, claimed that Debierue hadn't carried irrationality out far enough to make his point irrevocably meaningless. Neither group denied the powerful impact of *No. One* on the art of the times.

"By 1925 Surrealism was no longer a potent art force—although it was revived in the thirties and rejuvenated in the early fifties. And the remaining Dadaists in 1925, those who hadn't joined André Breton, were largely disorganized. Nevertheless, Debierue's exhibit was still a strong attraction right up until the day it closed. And it was popular enough with Americans to be included on two different guided tours of Paris offered by tourist agencies.

"Once Nihilistic Surrealism became established as an independent art movement, Debierue was in demand as a speaker. He turned these offers down, naturally—"

"Naturally? Doesn't a speaker usually get paid?"

"Yes, and he would've been well paid. But an artist doesn't put himself in a defensive position. And that's what happens to a speaker. A critic's supposed to speak. He welcomes questions, because his job is to explain what the artist does. The artist is untrained for this sort of thing, and all he does is weaken his position. Some painters go around the country on lecture tours today, carrying racks of slides of their work, and they're an embarrassed, inarticulate lot. The money's hard to turn down, I suppose, but in the end they defeat themselves and negate their work. A creative artist has no place on the lecture platform, and that goes for poets and novelists, as well as painters."

"So much for the Letters section of *The New York Review of Books.*"

"That's right. At least for poets and novelists. The nonfiction writer is entitled to lecture. He started an argument on purpose when he wrote his book, and he has every right to defend it. But the painter's work says what it has to say, and the critic interprets it for those who can't read it."

"In that case, you're responsible to the artist as well as to the public."

"I know. That's what I've been talking about. But it's a challenge, too, and that's why I'm so excited about interviewing Debierue. When Debierue was preparing to leave Paris, following the closing of his shop and exhibit, he granted an interview to a reporter from *Paris Soir*. He didn't say anything about his proposed work in progress, except to state that his painting was too private in meaning for either his intimate friends or the general public. He had decided, he said, not to show any of his future work to the general public, nor to any art critic he considered unqualified to write intelligently about his painting.

"For the 'qualified' critic, in other words, if not for the general public, the door was left ajar.

"The villa on the Riviera had been an anonymous gift to the artist, and he had accepted it in the spirit in which it was offered. No strings attached. He wasn't well-to-do, but the sale of his Montmartre shop would take care of his expenses for several months. The *Paris Soir* reporter then asked the obvious question. 'If you refuse to exhibit or to sell your paintings, how will you live?'

" 'That,' Debierue replied, 'isn't my concern. An artist has too much work to do to worry about such matters.' With his mistress clinging to his arm, Debierue climbed into a waiting taxi and was off to the railroad station.

"Perhaps it was the naivete of his reply that agitated an immediate concern among the painters he had known and befriended. At any rate, an organization named *Les Amis de Debierue* was formed hastily, within the month following his departure from the city. It's never disbanded."

"There was an organization like that formed for T. S. Eliot, but it disbanded. The purpose was to get Mr. Eliot out of his job at the bank."

"I know. But Eliot took another job in publishing. Debierue, so far as we know, never made another picture frame, except for his own work. *Les Amis* held its first fundraising banquet in Paris, and through this continuing activity enough money was collected to give the artist a small annual subsidy. Other donations are still solicited from art lovers annually. I've been giving *Les Amis de Debierue* at least five bucks a year since I left graduate school.

"During World War Two, the Germans let Debierue alone. Thanks to two critical articles that had linked his name with Nietzsche, he wasn't considered as a 'degenerate' French artist. And apparently they didn't discover any of his current work to examine for 'flaws.'

"When the Riviera was liberated, it was immediately transformed into an R and R area for U.S. troops, and he was soon visited by art students, now in uniform, who'd read about him in college. They mentioned him in their letters home, and it didn't take long for American art groups to begin a fresh flow of clothing, food, art supplies, and money to his Riviera outpost.

"Debierue had survived two world wars, and a dozen ideological battles.

"The first three reviews of Debierue's Riviera works, with a nod to *symbolisme*, are self-explanatory. 'Fantasy,' 'Oblique,' and 'Rain' are the names given to his first three 'periods'—as assigned by the first three critics who were allowed to examine his paintings. The fourth period, 'Chironesque,' is so hermetic it requires some amplification."

Berenice nodded in assent.

"A paucity of scholastic effort was put into the examination of these four important essays. Little has been published, either in book or monograph form as in-depth studies of each period—the way

Picasso's Rose and Blue periods have been covered. This is understandable, because the public never saw any of these pictures.

"The established critic prefers to examine the original work, or at least colored slides of that work, before he reaches his own conclusions. To refute or to agree with the critic who's seen the work puts a man on shaky ground. Each new article, as it appeared, however, received considerable attention. But writers were chary of making any expanded judgments based upon the descriptions alone."

"Yes, I can understand that."

"This general tendency didn't hold true for Louis Galt's essay, 'Debierue: The Chironesque Period,' which appeared in the Summer, 1958, *The Nonobjectivist*. It was reprinted in more than a dozen languages and art journals.

"Galt, you see, was known as an avowed purist in his approach to nonobjective art, and that's why he published his article in *The Nonobjectivist* when he could've had it published by *Art News* for ten times as much money. Galt had once gone so far as to call Mondrian a 'traitor' in print when the Dutchman gave up his black-and-white palette to experiment with color in his linear paintings. I didn't agree with him there, but he made some telling points. But with so many able critics available, all of them anxious to see Debierue's post–World War Two work, it was considered a damned shame that he'd chosen a purist who would only look at the new work from a prejudiced viewpoint.

"The appellation 'Chironesque' was considered as a derogatory 'literary' term. It was deeply resented by Susan Sontag, who said so in *The Partisan Review*. The Galt essay wasn't, in all fairness, disrespectful, but Galt stated bluntly that Debierue had retrogressed. He claimed that 'bicephalous centaurlike creatures' were clearly visible in the dozen paintings Debierue had shown him. And this forced Galt to conclude that the 'master' was now a 'teacher,' and that didacticism had no place in contemporary art. The 'purist' view, of course."

"Of course." Berenice nodded.

"At any rate—and here he was reaching for it—because Chiron the centaur was the mythical teacher of Hercules, and other Greek heroes, Galt christened the period 'Chironesque.' This was a cunning allusion to the classicism Galt detested, elements Galt would've considered regressive in any modern painter.

"Debierue, of course, said nothing."

Berenice nodded and closed her eyes.

"The controversial Galt essay was well timed. It rejuvenated interest in the old painter, and the 'bicephalous centaurlike creatures,' as described by Galt, made the new work resemble—or appear to resemble—Abstract Expressionism. Some wishful thinking was going on. Nineteen fifty-eight wasn't an exciting pictorial year. Except for a handful of New York painters, called the 'Sidney Janis Painters,' after their dealer, the so-called New York School was undergoing a transitional phase. And Debierue was news, of course, because he'd received so little public notice in recent years."

Berenice dropped her chin. "Uh huh."

"One New York dealer cabled Debierue an offer of fifty thousand dollars for any one of the Chironesque paintings, sight unseen. Debierue acknowledged it by sending back a blank cablegram—with just his type signature. The dealer took advantage of the publicity by blowing up a copy of his offer and Debierue's reply and by placing the photo blow-ups in the window of his Fifty-seventh Street gallery. Other dealers, who aped and upped the original offer, didn't receive any replies.

"How I'll manage it, I don't know, Berenice. I know only that I'm determined to be the first critic to see Debierue's American paintings, and I've already decided to call it his 'American Period'!"

But I was talking to myself. Berenice, I noticed, with some irritation, had fallen asleep.

6

DESPITE HER SIZE, and she was a large woman, Berenice, curled and cramped up in sleep, looked vulnerable to the point of fragility. Her unreasonably long blond lashes swept round flushed cheeks, and her childish face, in repose and without makeup, took several years from her age. Her heavy breasts and big round ass, however, exposed now, as the short flimsy nightgown rode high above her hips, were incongruously mature in contrast with her innocent face and tangled Alice-in-Wonderland hair. As I examined her, with squinty-eyed, ambivalent interest, a delicate bubble of spit formed in the exact center of her bowed, slightly parted lips.

Oh, I had put Berenice to sleep all right, with my discursive discussion of Jacques Debierue. With an impatient, involuntary yawn of my own I wondered how much she had understood about Debierue before she had drifted off completely. She had been attentive, of course, as she always was when I talked to her, but she had never asked a serious question. Not that it made much difference. Berenice had a minimal interest in art—or in anything that bordered on abstract thought—and for some time I had suspected that the slight interest she was able to muster occasionally was largely feigned. An effort to please me.

Except for her adhesive interest in me as a person, or personality, and in matching sexual frequencies, I wondered if anything else had ever stimulated her intellectually. For a woman who had majored in English, and taught the subject (granted, she taught on a high school level), she was surprisingly low on insight into the nature of literature.

No one could accuse her of being well read, either. Her insights into literature when I had, on occasion, attempted to draw her out, were either sophomoric or parroted generalities remembered from her college English courses. She had an excellent memory for plot lines and the names of characters, but for little else.

She was probably a poor classroom teacher, I decided. She had such a lazy good-natured disposition she could not have been any great shakes as a disciplinarian. But she would have few disciplinary problems in a city like Duluth, where teenagers were polite incipient Republicans. New York high school students would have had a gentle woman like Berenice in tears within minutes.

But how did I know? I didn't. In a power situation, with children, she might inspire terror, fear, and trembling. She never talked about her work and, for all I knew, she might be an expert in grammar and a veritable hotshot in the classroom.

The persona of a woman in love is highly deceiving.

Did she feign sentimentality as well as other things? She cried real tears one night when Timmy Fraser sang "My Funny Valentine" at the Red Pirate Lounge—stretching out the song in the mournful way that he does for fully ten minutes. Any woman who fails to recognize the inherent viciousness of Lorenz Hart's 1930s lyrics has a head filled with cornmeal stirabout instead of brains. She also mentioned once that she had cried for two days over Madame Bovary's suicide. Fair enough. Flaubert had earned those tears, but she had no insight into the style of the novel, nor did she analyze how Flaubert had maneuvered her emotionally into weeping over the death of that poor, sick woman.

Knowing this much, and after thinking about it, I realized that I knew very little about her, it was unreasonable of me to expect a wakeful interest from Berenice in Jacques Debierue. Berenice was a funny valentine, that is what she was, and her chin was a little weak, too. In a vague abstract way I loved her. At the same time, I wondered what to do with her. She had been a sounding board to diminish some of the excitement inside me, but now it was two A.M. and I was going to be busy today. Busy, busy. Perhaps if I used her right, she would be an asset. Wouldn't it help to have a beautiful woman in tow when I called on Debierue? He would hardly slam the door in the face of a strikingly attractive woman. A Frenchman? Never . . .

The bubble of spit ballooned suddenly as she exhaled, and inaudibly popped. Berenice whimpered in her sleep and tried, wriggling, to find a more comfortable position in her chair. This was impossible. With her long legs cramped up under her rear and in a tight-fitting canvas officer's chair, it was miraculous that she could fall asleep in the first place.

I stopped rationalizing, recognizing what I was doing—rationalizing—and prodded Berenice's soft but rather flat belly with a stiff forefinger.

"Wake up, Audience," I said, not unkindly.

"I wasn't asleep," she lied. "I just closed my eyes for a second to rest them."

"I know. I forgot to ask, but where have you been the last couple of days?"

"Here." Her eyes widened. "Right here."

"Not today you weren't."

"Oh, you mean today?"

"Yes. Today."

"I was at Gloria's apartment. Honestly, I got so blue just sitting around here all alone waiting for you to come back that I called her. She drove over for me and took me in."

"I thought as much. Gloria tried to pump me on the phone when I got back. I thought something was odd about her phony laughter, but couldn't figure it out. If you didn't intend to go back to Duluth, why did you take your bags and leave that weird note for me?"

"I tried to go, I really did, but I just couldn't!" Her eyes moistened. "I want to stay with you, James . . . don't you want me to?"

I had to forestall her tears. Why can't women learn how to say "Good-bye" like a man?

"We'll see, baby, we'll see. Let's go to bed now. We'll talk about it in the morning, much later *this* morning."

Berenice rose obediently, crossed her arms, and with a sweeping, graceful movement removed her shorty nightgown. No longer sleepy, she grinned wickedly and crawled onto the tumbled Murphy bed, shaking her tremendous stern as she did so. I smiled. She was amusing when she tried to be coy because she was so big. I undressed slowly and crawled in beside her. The air-conditioner, without enough BTUs to cool the apartment adequately, labored away—uh uh, uh uh, uh uh. . . . As a rule I could shut the sound out, but now it bothered me.

I was tense, slightly high from drinking four cups of black coffee, and overstimulated by my ability to recall, with so little effort, the details of Debierue's career. Three, no, four days had passed since the last time, and yet, strangely, I wasn't interested in sex. To make love now would be to initiate a new beginning to a something I had written "ending" to—perhaps that was the reason. That, or my unresolved feelings about Berenice now that I was on the verge of a future—if everything worked out all right—that held no place for a woman who was interested in me as a person. Any relationship between a man and a woman that is based upon bodies and personalities alone can lead only to disaster.

It was a premonition, or some kind of precognitive instinct for self-preservation, I should have heeded. But at two in the morning, with my mind still reeling with matters intellectual, I was physically unable to muster enough brute bellicosity to toss Berenice and her suitcase down the stairs. She was loving, too loving.

The inchoate premonition, or whatever it was, of some disaster, froze my body as well as my mind into a state of flaccid inaction. Berenice was puzzled, I know. When none of her usual tricks worked, she climbed over me suddenly, got out of bed, and switched off the floor lamp. Except for the tiny red light on the electric coffee-pot, which was not a red, baleful staring eye, but merely an effective reminder that the coffee was hot if I was not, the room was as dark as my thoughts. We had never made love in the dark before. I didn't know about Berenice, but such a peculiar idea had never occurred to me in my lifetime. It is too impersonal to make love in the dark. Your partner could be *anyone,* anyone at all.

How she knew this I don't know, but the gimmick worked. As Berenice whipped her head back and forth, stinging first my chest and then my stomach with her long hair, my doubts disappeared. And because this unseen woman became any woman, and was no longer a problem named Berenice Hollis, I became rigid with the pain of need, and mounted her savagely. Savagely for me, because I am usually methodical in sexual relations, knowing what I like and dislike. Being flagellated with long hair was a new experience for me as well, and I favored Berenice with the best ride she had ever had. She climaxed as I entered, then twice, and we made the final one together. She bit my shoulder so hard to keep from mewing (knowing how irritated I get when she makes animal noises) she left the marks of her teeth in my skin.

Euphoric, my tenseness dissipated, the thought of sending this big, marvelous woman back to Minnesota became intolerable. She turned on the floorlamp and rummaged around in her suitcase for douching equipment.

"Hang up that yellow linen suit of yours, baby," I told her, "so the wrinkles will shake out."

"Why?" she asked, doing as she was told. "It isn't wrinkled."

"Because I want you to wear it tomorrow. I'm taking you with me."

"Where are we going? Are we going to have fun?"

"To call on M. Debierue." I sighed. "I'll try to explain it again tomorrow—in one-syllable words." With the light on, Berenice Hollis was a problem again.

"We'll have fun, though, won't we?"

"Sure," I replied glumly. "Fun, fun, fun."

I closed my eyes as she went into the bathroom. I remember dimly being washed with a warm washrag, but I was sound asleep before she finished.

PART TWO

If Anything Exists, It Is Incomprehensible

1

THE APARTMENT LOOKED terrible, as if a small whirlwind had been turned loose for a few minutes, but Berenice, in her lemon linen suit, with its skimpy microskirt, was beautiful. At my request she wore stockings, sheer enough to enhance the sienna brown of her deeply tanned legs. The skirt was so short, when she sat or leaned over, the white metal snaps that held up her stockings were exposed slyly enough to make her as sexy as a Varga drawing.

Instead of a blouse she wore a filmy blue-and-red scarf around her neck. The two loose ends of the scarf were tucked crosswise beneath the lapels of the square-cut double-breasted jacket. Very few women would dare to wear such a severely cut suit, but the square straight lines of the jacket exaggerated the roundness of Berenice's lush figure. With the supplement of a rat she had put up her hair, and the ample mound of tawny hair, sun-tinged with yellow streaks, piled on top of her head, together with her childish features, gave her an angelic expression.

There was, I think, too much orange in her lipstick, but perhaps this slight imperfection was the single needed touch that made her so lovely as a whole.

I had shaved and showered before Berenice took over the bathroom for an hour, and I had trimmed my Spanish Don sideburns neatly with scissors. Nevertheless, I looked incongruously raunchy beside Berenice in my faded blue denim, short-sleeved jumpsuit, especially when she slipped on a pair of white gloves. It was too hot outside for a jacket, and I needed the multiple pockets in the jumpsuit to carry all my paraphernalia.

I had three pens, a notebook, my wallet and keys, a handkerchief, two packs of Kools, and my ribbed-model Dunhill lighter (one of the few luxuries I had treated myself to when I had a regular teaching salary coming in), a tiny Kodak Bantam in my right trousers pocket, some loose change, a pocket magnifying glass in a leather case, fingernail clippers, and a two-inch piece of clammy jade, with indentations for a finger grip. Except for the well-concealed Kodak Bantam, loaded with color film, I carried too much crap around with me, but I had gotten used to carrying it and could hardly do without it.

We had slept late and had a leisurely breakfast. After getting dressed, I had jotted down a few questions in my notebook. I would not refer to the questions, but the act of writing them down had set them in my mind. This was an old reporter's trick that worked, and I always took my Polaroid camera along, loaded with black-and-white, and extra film. Professionals sneer at Dr. Edwin H. Land's Polaroids, but I was an expert with them and rarely snapped more than two shots before getting what I wanted. I had learned, too, that people will okay without argument almost any picture that they have seen, but will refuse to allow photos to be published when they haven't seen everything on the roll.

By 1:30 p.m. we were ready to go. I preceded Berenice down the stairs into the glare of the breathtaking Florida sunlight. The humidity was close to ninety, although the temperature wasn't quite eighty-five. There were threatening nimbus clouds farther south, but the sky was clear and blue above Palm Beach. It doesn't always rain in South Florida when the humidity hits 100 percent, although technically it is supposed to, but inasmuch as we were heading toward the dark sky above Boynton Beach, I decided not to put the canvas top back. Inside the car, on burning leatherette seats, we sweltered.

We had hardly crossed the bridge into West Palm when Berenice pointed to a blazing orange roof and said, "Let's stop at Howard Johnson's."

"Why? We just finished breakfast an hour ago."

"I have to widdle. That's why."

"I told you to pee before we left."

"I did, but I have to go again."

It was partly the heat, but I jerked the car into the parking lot, thinking angrily that it wasn't too late. I could call a cab and send Berenice back to the apartment.

But once inside the cave-cold depths and booth-seated, I ordered two chocolate ice cream sodas, waited for them and Berenice, and smoked a Kool. Because the service was seasonal, Berenice joined me at the table long before the sodas arrived. She picked up my cigarette from the ashtray, took a long drag, replaced the cigarette exactly as she found it, held the inhaled smoke inside her lungs like a skin diver trying to break the hold-your-breath-underwater record, and finally let what was left of the smoke out. I had noticed, during the three days I was in Miami, when Berenice had not been with me, that her so-called efforts to quit smoking caused three packs a day to go up in smoke instead of my usual two. She had merely quit buying and carrying them. She smoked mine instead—or took long drags off the cigarette I happened to be smoking. She hated mentholated cigarettes, or so she claimed, but not enough, apparently, to give them up altogether.

"If you want a cigarette," I said, pushing the pack toward her, "take one. When you drag mine down a quarter of an inch that way, I finish the cigarette unsatisfied because I didn't have the exact ration of smoke I'm accustomed to. Then, because I feel gypped out of a quarter inch, I light another one, only to find that an entire cigarette, smoked too soon after the one I just finished, is too much. I butt it, replace it in the pack, and when I finally get around to lighting the butt the next time I want a smoke, it tastes too strong and it still isn't a regular-length smoke. If I throw the butt away, with only a couple of drags gone, it's a waste, and—"

Berenice put a cool hand over mine. There were faint crinkles in the corners of her guileless cornflower blue eyes. Her bowed lips narrowed as they flickered a rapid smile.

"What's bothering you, James?"

I shrugged. "I don't know. I took an up with my third cup of coffee, and the combination of a benny with too much coffee makes me talk too much. As I told you last night, Berenice, this is a one-of-a-kind opportunity for me. And I'm apprehensive, that's all."

She shook her head. The smile appeared and disappeared again so fast I almost missed it. "No, James, you told me so much about this painter last night I got confused, bogged down in details, so to speak. Something is either missing or you didn't tell me everything."

"You fell asleep, for Christ's sake."

"No, I didn't. Well, maybe toward the end. But what I don't understand is how this painter, this Debierue, can be such a famous painter when no one has ever seen any of his paintings. It doesn't make sense."

"What do you mean, no one has seen his paintings? Thousands of people saw his first one-man show, and his subsequent work has been written about by Mazzeo, Charonne, Reinsberg, and Galt, who all studied his paintings. These are some of the most famous critics of this century, for God's sake!"

She shook her head and pursed her lips. "I don't mean them, or even you—that is, if you get to see what he's painted since coming to Florida. I mean the public, the people who flock to museums when a traveling Van Gogh show comes in, and buy all kinds of Van Gogh reproductions and so on. I had seen dozens of Van Gogh paintings in books and magazines long before I ever saw one of his originals. That's what I mean by famous. How can I be impressed by Debierue's fame when I've never seen any of his work and can't judge for myself how good he is?"

Our ice cream sodas arrived. I didn't want to hurt Berenice's feelings, but I was forced to because of her ignorance.

"Look, baby, you aren't qualified to judge for yourself. Now keep quiet, and drink your nice ice cream soda—there's a good girl—and I'll try and explain it to you. Did you ever study cetology?"

"I don't know. What is it?"

"The scientific study of whales. A cetologist is a man who studies whales, and he can spend an entire lifetime at it, just as I've spent my life, so far, studying art—as have the critics who wrote about Debierue. Now, let's suppose that you pick up a copy of *Scientific American* and read an article about whales written by a well-known cetologist—"

"Are there any well-known cetologists?"

"There are bound to be. I don't have any names to rattle off for you—that isn't my racket. But I haven't finished yet. All right, you're reading this article by a cetologist in *Scientific American* and he states that a baby sperm whale is a tail presentation."

"What does that mean?"

"It means that a baby whale, unlike other mammals, is born tail first."

"How do you know that?"

"I read a lot. But the same would hold true even if the cetologist said that it was a cephalic presentation. The point I'm making is this: The article is written by a cetologist and published in *Scientific American,* and you will accept an expert's word for it. You aren't going to get yourself a goddamned boat and sail around the seven fucking seas trying to find a pregnant whale, are you? Just so you can check on whether a baby whale is born head first or tail first?"

Berenice giggled. "You're cute when you're stern. No . . . I guess not, but art, it seems to me, is supposed to be for everybody, not just for those critics you mentioned . . ."

I put down the spoon and wiped my lips on a paper napkin. "*Whales* are for everybody, too, sweetheart. But not everybody studies whales as a lifetime occupation. That's the big difference you don't seem to understand."

"All right." She shrugged. "I still think there's something you haven't told me about all this."

I grinned. "There is. In return for Debierue's address I've got to do a favor for Mr. Cassidy—"

"The lawyer who told you about Debierue?"

"Yeah." I nodded. "And what I'm telling you is 'privileged information,' as Cassidy would put it. It's between you and Mr. Cassidy and these ice cream sodas."

"You can trust me, James." Her face softened. "You can trust me with your life."

"I know. And in a way it *is* my life. Anyway, Mr. Cassidy gave me privileged information—where Debierue is living—and all I have to do in return is to steal a picture for him."

"Steal a picture? Why can't he buy one? He's rich enough."

"Debierue doesn't sell his pictures. I explained all that. If Cassidy gets a picture, even one that's been stolen, he'll be the only collector in the world to have one, you see."

"What good will it do him? If it's a stolen picture, Debierue can get it back by calling the police."

"Debierue won't know he has it, and neither will anyone else—until after Debierue's dead, anyway. Then the picture will be even more valuable."

"How're you going to steal a picture without Debierue knowing it was you?"

"I don't know yet. I'm playing things by ear at the moment. It might not be a picture. If he's working with ceramics, I can slip a piece in my pocket while you distract him. Maybe there are some drawings around. Mr. Cassidy would be satisfied with a drawing. In fact he'd be delighted. But until I find out what Debierue has been doing, I won't know what to do myself."

"But you want me to help you?"

"If you want to, yes. He can't watch both of us at the same time, and he's an old man. So when a chance comes, and it will, I'll give you the high sign and then I'll snatch something."

"It's awfully haphazard, James, the way you say it. Besides, as soon as we leave, he'll know that you're the one who stole it—what*ever* it is."

"No." I shook my head. "He won't know. He'll *suspect* that I took it, but he won't be able to prove it. I'll deny everything, if charged, and besides it'll never get that far. Meanwhile, Mr. Cassidy will have the painting, chunk of sculpture, drawing, or whatever, hidden away where Jesus Christ couldn't find it. See?"

"Do you realize, James," she said, rather primly, "that if you ever got caught stealing a painting from anybody that your career would be over?"

"Not really, and not, certainly, from Debierue. His work, as you mentioned before about Van Gogh, belongs to the world—and if I were ever tried for something like that, which I wouldn't be—I'd have a defense fund from art lovers and art magazines that would make me look like a White Panther. Anyway, that's the plan—in addition to somehow getting an interview, of course."

"It isn't much of a plan."

"True. But now that you know what I have to do, you might get an idea once we're on the scene. The important thing is this: don't take anything yourself. I'll take it when the time is propitious. I have to get the interview before anything else is done."

"I understand."

The rain caught us before we reached Lake Worth.

There were torrents of it, and I could hardly see to drive. Berenice, because of her suit, had to roll up her window, but it was too hot for me to roll up mine. My left shoulder and arm got soaked, but with the humidity I would have been just as wet inside the car with the window rolled up. The rain finally came down so hard I had to pull over to the curb in Lake Worth to wait for a letup.

Berenice was frowning. "How much," she asked, "does a baby whale weigh when it's first born?"

"One ton. And it's fourteen feet long." I lit a cigarette and passed it to Berenice. She shook her head and handed it back. I took a long drag. "One ton," I said solemnly, "is two thousand pounds."

"I *know* how much a ton is!" she said angrily. "You—you—you damned intellectual, you!"

I couldn't contain myself. I had to laugh and ruin my joke.

2

COULD HAVE TAKEN State Road Seven straight away by picking it up west of West Palm Beach, but because the old two-lane highway was used primarily by truck traffic barreling for Miami's back door, into Hialeah, I stayed on U.S. 1 all the way to Boynton Beach before searching for a through road to make the cutover. I got lost for a few minutes and made several aimless circles where new blacktops had been crushed down for a subdivision called inappropriately Ocean Pine Terraces (miles from the ocean, no pines, no terraces), but when I finally reached the state highway, it was freshly paved, and the truck traffic wasn't nearly as bad as I had expected.

The rain, mercifully, had stopped.

My crude map was clear enough, but I had zipped past Debierue's turnoff to the Dixie Drive-in Movie Theater before I realized it. The mixed dirt-and-gravel private road leading to Debierue's home-and-studio was clearly visible from the highway, and on the right of the highway about three hundred yards before the drive-in entrance, but I had failed to notice it. I made a crimped circle in the deserted drive-in entrance and this time, from the other side of the highway, it was easy to spot the break.

Thick gama grass had reclaimed the deep wheel ruts of the road, and I crawled along in first gear. The bumpy, rarely used trail straight-lined through a stand of second-growth slash pine for about a half mile and then made a sigmoid loop to circumvent two stinking stagnant ponds of black swamp water. On the right of the road, abandoned chicken runs stretched into the jungly mass of greenery, and weeds had grown straight and tall along the sagging chicken-wire fences. The unpainted wooden chickenhouses had weathered to an unpatterned dirty gray, and most of the roofs had caved in. The narrow road petered out at an open peeled-pine gate. I eased into the fenced area, with its untended, thickly grassed yard, which resembled a huge, brown bathmat, and pulled up in front of the screened porch of the house.

Paradoxically, I was awed by my first sight of the old painter. I switched off the engine, and as it ticked heatedly away, I sat and stared. I say "paradoxically" because Debierue in person was anything but awe inspiring.

He resembled any one of a thousand, no literally tens of thousands, of those tanned Florida retirees one sees on bridges fishing, on golf courses tottering, and on the shuffleboard courts of rest homes and public parks shuffling. He even wore the uniform. Green-billed khaki baseball cap, white denim Bermuda shorts, low-cut Zayre tennis shoes in pale blue canvas, and the standard white open-necked "polo" shirt with short sleeves. The inevitable tiny green alligator was embroidered over the left pocket of the shirt, an emblem so common in Florida that any Miami Beach comedian could get a laugh by saying, "They caught an alligator in the Glades the other day, and he was wearing a shirt with a little man sewn over the pocket . . ."

But unlike those other thousands of old men who had retired to Florida in anticipation of a warm death, men who had earned their dubious retirement by running shoe stores, managing light-bulb plants in Amarillo, manufacturing condoms in Newark, hustling as harried sales managers in the ten western states, Debierue had served, and was still serving, the strictest master of them all—the self-discipline of the artist.

Debierue, apparently unperturbed by the arrival of a strange, beat-up convertible in his yard, sat limberly erect in a green-webbed, aluminum patio chair beside the porch door, soaking up late afternoon sun. I was pleased to see that he was allowing his white beard to grow again (for several years he had been clean shaven), but it was not as long and Melvillean as it had been in photos of the old artist taken in the twenties.

Physically, Debierue was asthenic. Long-limbed, long-bodied, slight, with knobby knees and elbows. Advanced age had caused his thin shoulders to droop, of course, and there was a melony potbelly below his belt. His sun-bronzed skin, although it was wrinkled, gave the old man a healthy, almost robust appearance. His keen blue eyes were alert and unclouded, and the great blade of his beaky French nose did not have those exposed, tiny red veins one usually associates with aged retirees in Florida. His full, sensuous lips formed a fat grape-colored "O"—a dark, plump circle encircled by white hair. His blue stare, with which he returned mine, was incurious, polite, direct, and distant, but during the long uncomfortable moment we sat in silent confrontation, I detected an air of vigilance in his sharp old eyes.

As a critic I had learned early in the game how unwise it was to give too much weight or credence to first impressions, but under his steady, unwavering gaze I felt—I *knew*—that I was in the presence of a giant, which, in turn, made me feel like a violator, a criminal. And if, in that first moment, he had pointed to the gate silently—without even saying "Get out!"—I would have departed without uttering a word.

But such was not the case.

Berenice, her hands folded in her lap over her chamois drawstring handbag, sat quietly, and there she would sit until I got out of the car, walked around it, and opened the door on her side.

I was uninvited, an unexpected visitor, and it was up to me to break the frozen sea that divided us. Apprehensively, and dangling the Land camera from its carrying strap on two fingers, I got out of the car and nodded politely.

"Good afternoon, M. Debierue," I said in French, trying to keep my voice deep, like Jean Gabin, "at long last we meet!"

Apparently he hadn't heard any French (and mine wasn't so bad) for a long time. Debierue smiled—and what a wonderful, warmhearted smile he had! His smile was so sweet, so sincere, so insinuating that my heart twisted with sudden pain. It was a smile to shatter the world. His age-ruined mouth, purple lips and all, was beautiful when he smiled. Several teeth were missing, both uppers and lowers, and those that remained gave a jack-o'-lantern effect to his generous mouth. But the swift transformation from mournful resignation to rejuvenated, unrestrained happiness changed his entire appearance. The grooved down-pointing lines in his face were twisted into swirling, upswept arabesques. He rose stiffly from his chair as I approached, and shook a long forefinger at me in mock reproach.

"Ah, M. Figueras! You have shaved your beard. You must grow it back quickly!"

His greeting me by name that way brought sudden moisture to my eyes. He pumped my hand, the single up-and-down European handshake. His long spatulate fingers were warm and dry.

"You—you *know* me?" I said, in unfeigned astonishment.

He treated me to the first in a series of bona fide Gallic shrugs. "You, or another—" he said mysteriously, "and it is well that it is you. I am familiar with your work, naturally, M. Figueras."

I gulped like a tongue-tied teenager, abashed, not knowing what to say, and then noticed that he was looking past my shoulder toward Berenice.

"Oh!" I said, running around the car, and helping Berenice out the door. "This is my friend, M. Debierue, Mlle Hollis."

Berenice glared at me when I pronounced her name "Holee," and said, "Hollis, Mr. Debierue," in English, "Berenice Hollis. And it's a pleasure to meet you, sir."

Debierue kissed her hand, and I thought (I was probably over-sensitive) he was a little uneasy, or put off by her presence. He didn't know—and there was no unawkward way for me to enlighten him—whether she was truly just a friend, my mistress, my secretary, or a well-heeled art patron. I decided to say nothing more. He would be able to tell for himself by the way she looked at me and touched my arm from time to time that we were on intimate terms. It was best to let it go at that.

The old man's English was adequate, despite a heavy accent, and as we talked in French, that beautiful late April afternoon, he or I occa-sionally translated or made some comment to Berenice in English.

"I'm one of those obscure journalists who presume to criticize art," I said modestly, with a nervous smile, but he stopped me by rais-ing a hand.

"Non, no, no"—he shook his head—"not obscure, M. Figueras. I know your work well. The article you wrote on the California painter . . . ?" He frowned.

"Vint? Ray Vint, you mean?"

"Yes, that's the name. The little fly. That was so droll." He chuckled reflectively. "Do not feel guilty, M. Figueras." He shrugged. "The true artist cannot hide forever, and if not you, another would come. Now, come! Come inside! I will give you cold orange juice, fresh frozen Minute Maid."

I was flattered that he knew my work as well as my name, or at least *one* article—I checked myself—written in English, at that, and not to my knowledge translated into French. But why did he mention this particular article on Vint? Ray Vint was an abstract painter whose paintings sold sparsely—for a dozen good reasons I won't go into here. Vint was an excellent craftsman, however, and could get all the portrait work he desired—more, in fact, than he wanted to paint. He needed the money he made from portraits to be able to work on the abstracts he preferred to paint. But because he hated to do portraits, he also hated the people who sat for them and provided him with large sums for flattering likenesses. He got "revenge" on the sitters by painting a fly on them.

In medieval painting, and well into the Renaissance, a fly was painted on Jesus Christ's crucified body: the fly on Jesus' body was a symbol of redemption, because a fly represented sin and Jesus was without sin. A fly painted on the person of a layman, however, signified sin *without* redemption, or translated into "This person is going to Hell!" Ray Vint painted a trompe-l'oeil fly on every portrait.

Sometimes his patrons didn't notice the fly for several days, and when they did they were unaware of its significance. They were usually delighted when they discovered it. The fly became a conversational gambit when they showed the portrait to their friends: "Notice anything unusual there about my portrait?"

Artists, of course, when they saw the fly, laughed inwardly, but said nothing to the patrons about the meaning of the Vintian trademark. I had hesitated about whether to mention Vint's symbolic revenge when I wrote about him, not wanting to jeopardize his livelihood. But I had decided, in the end, to bring the matter up because it was a facet of Vint's personality that said something implicit about the emotionless nature of his abstracts.

As I guided Berenice into the house in Debierue's wake, holding her left elbow, I became apprehensive about the old painter's offhand remark and dry, brief chuckle. A chuckle, unlike a sudden smile or a sincere burst of laughter, is difficult to interpret. Whether a chuckle is friendly or unfriendly, it merely serves as a nervous form of punctuation. But to mention one particular incident, or paragraph, out of the thousands I had written, and the "fly" symbol at that, caused the knot of anxiety in the pit of my stomach to throb. The fact that he had read my piece on Vint (not a hack job, because I don't write hack pieces, but it certainly wasn't one of my best articles—Vint's work simply hadn't been good enough for a serious in-depth treatment) could be a hindrance to me.

No one knew, because Debierue had never commented, what the old man had thought about Galt's article, with its fanciful "Chironesque" interpretations, but writers with reputations much greater than mine had been turned down subsequently when they had asked the painter for interviews. After the Galt article, Debierue had every right to distrust critics.

Damn Galt, anyway, I thought bitterly. Then I saw the gilded baroque frame on the wall and pointed to it.

"That isn't the famous *No. One,* is it?"

Debierue pursed his lips, and shrugged. "It was," he answered lightly, and entered the kitchen.

The moment I examined the picture I knew what he meant, of course. There was no crack on the wall behind the mount. The frame, without the crack, and not hanging in its original environment, was no longer the fabled *No. One.* My exultation was great nevertheless. It was something I had never expected to see in my lifetime. Berenice, after a quick glance at the empty frame, seated herself in a Sears-Danish chair and asked me for a cigarette.

I shook my head impatiently. "Not till we ask permission," I told her.

There was a narrow bar-counter built into the wall. It separated the kitchen from the living room. There was no dining room, and the living room was furnished Spartanly. The chicken farmer-tenant who had built the house had probably intended, like many Floridians, to use the large screened porch as a dining area. There was a square, confirming pass-through window from the kitchen to the porch.

There were no other pictures on the walls, and the living room was furnished cheaply and austerely with Sears furniture. Mr. Cassidy had certainly spared expense in furnishing the house for the famous visitor. There wasn't a hi-fi stereo, a radio, or television set, and there were no drapes to mask the severe horizontal lines of the Venetian blinds covering the windows. Except for two Danish chairs, a Marfak-topped coffee table, a black Naugahyde two-seater couch, and one floor lamp—all grouped in a tight oblong—the huge living room, with its carpetless terrazzo floor, was bare. A *Miami Herald* and a superslick copy of *Réalités* were on the coffee table. There were two tall black wrought-iron barstools at the counter. Debierue either had to have his meals at this bar-counter or take his food out to the porch and eat on a Samsonite card table.

Mr. Cassidy would not, I knew, tip Debierue off that I was coming, but if the old painter asked me how I had found him, what could I say? He didn't appear surprised by my sudden appearance. If he asked, I would say that my editor had told me and that he sent me down on an assignment. These thoughts nagged at my mind as Debierue prepared the frozen orange juice. He placed an aluminum pitcher on the table, opened the frozen can with an electric can opener, and then made three trips to the sink to fill the empty can with tap water.

He worked methodically, with great concentration, adding each canful of water to the pitcher like a chemist preparing an experiment. With a long-handled spoon he stirred the mixture, smiled, and beckoned for us to come and sit at the bar. Berenice and I climbed onto the stools, and he filled three plastic glasses to their brims.

Without touching his glass he looked beyond me to *No. One* on the wall. "This is the new world, M. Figueras, and there are no cracks in the wall of the new world. Here the concrete, brick, and stucco walls are hurricane-proof. My insurance policy guarantees this."

This might be a good opening or closing sentence for my article, I thought. I leaned forward, prepared to explore his thinking on the "new world" in more detail, but he shook his head as a signal for me to remain silent.

"I will not suggest to you that only M. Cassidy could have directed you here, M. Figueras. It is unimportant now that you are here, and we are both aware that M. Cassidy is, like all collectors, a most peculiar man."

Grateful for the easy out, I asked for permission to smoke. Debierue took a saucer from the cabinet, set it between us, and waited until I lighted Berenice's cigarette and mine before he continued. He refused a cigarette by waving his hand.

"What can I say to you, M. Figueras, that would dissuade you from writing about me for your magazine?"

"Nothing, I'm afraid. You make me feel like a complete bastard, but—"

"I'm sorry for your feelings. But as a favor to me, do you have so much zeal that you must tell my address in your magazine? Much privacy is needed for my work, as it is for all artists. Every day I must work for at least four hours, and to have frequent interruptions—"

"That's no concession at all, sir. I'll dateline my piece 'Somewhere in Florida.' I know how you feel, of course. The Galt article was damned unfair to you, I know—"

"How do you know?" Again the sad, sweet smile.

"I know Galt's attitude toward art, that's how I know. He's got a one-track mental set. He invariably puts everything he sees into a highly subjective pattern—whether it fits or not.

"Is not all art subjective?"

"Yes." I grinned. "But didn't Braque say that the subject was not the object?"

"Perhaps. I don't know whether Braque said this himself, or whether some clever young man—a man like yourself, M. Figueras—*said* that he said it."

"I—I don't recall," I replied lamely, "where the quote originated, not at the moment, but he is supposed to have said it himself. And if not . . . well . . . the play on words has a subtle validity, for . . . the art of our times. Don't you think . . . ?"

"The word 'validity' cannot be used validly for the art of any time."

I hesitated. He was testing me. By going into theoretical entelechy I could have answered him easily, but I didn't want to argue with him—I shrugged and smiled.

"By validity," he smiled back, "do you mean that the eye contains the incipient action?" The corners of his eyes wrinkled with amusement.

"Not exactly, sir. Cartesian dualism, as an approach to aesthetics, no longer has intrinsic value—and that's Galt's fault. He has never been able to transcend his early training. Not to be summational is the hardest task facing the contemporary critic. To see the present alone, blocking out the past and future, calls for optic mediation." My face grew warm under the force of his steady blue eyes. "I don't mean to run Galt down, sir, or to give you the impression that I'm a better critic than he is. It's just that I'm twenty-five years younger than Galt, and I've looked at more contemporary art than he has—"

"Do not be so nervous, M. Figueras. *(?)Debemos dar preferencia al hablar del español?*"

"No. I think in Spanish when I speak it, and I prefer to think in English and talk in French—"

"What are you talking about?" Berenice said, sipping from her glass.

CHARLES WILLEFORD

"The difference between Spanish and English and French," I said.

"I hate Spanish," Berenice said, winking at me. "It's got too many words for bravery, which makes a person wonder sometimes about the true bravery of the Spanish character."

"And French, I think," Debierue said in English, "has too many words for love." He reached over and touched my hair. "You have nice curly yellow hair, and she should not tease you. Come now, drink your orange juice."

The paternal touch of his hand unknotted my inner tenseness, and I realized that the old artist was trying to make things easier for me. At any rate, my guilty feelings had been dissipated by his casual acceptance of both me and my professionalism. My awe of the old painter was also going away. I was still mightily impressed by him, and I felt that our conversation was going well.

Any writer who is awed in the presence of the great or the near-great cannot function critically. I respected Debierue enough to be wary, however, knowing that he was not an ingenuous man, knowing that he had survived as an individual all of these years by maintaining an aloof, if not an arrogant, silence, and a studied indifference to journalists. Debierue realized, I think, that I was on his side, and that I would always take an artist's viewpoint before that of the insensitive public's. He had read my work and he remembered my name. I could therefore give him credit for knowing that I was as unbiased as any art critic can ever be. To see his paintings, which was the major reason for my odyssey, I now had to gain his complete confidence. I had to guard against my tendency to argue. Nor should I bait him merely to obtain a few sensational opinions about art as "news."

"I am curious about why you immigrated to Florida, M. Debierue."

"I almost didn't. For my old bones, I wanted the sun. When more than fifty years of my work was burned in the fire—you knew about the fire?"

"Yes, sir."

"A most fortunate accident. It gave me a chance to begin again. The artist who can begin again at my age is a very fortunate man. So it was to the new world I turned, the new world and a new start. Tahiti, I think at first, would be best, but my name would then be linked somehow to Gauguin." He shook his head sadly. "Unavoidable. Such comparisons would not be fair, but they would have been made. And on the small island, perhaps the bus would pass my studio every day with American tourists to stare at me. Tahiti, no. Then I think, South America? No, there is always trouble there. And then Florida seems exactly right. But I did not come right away. I knew about the war in Florida, and I have had enough war in my lifetime."

"The war?" I said, puzzled. "The war in Vietnam?"

"No, no. The Seminole War. It is well known in Europe that these, the Florida Seminole Indians, are at war with your United States. Is it not so?"

"Yes, I suppose so, but only in a technical sense. The Seminoles are actually a very small Indian nation. And it's not a real war. It's a failure on the part of the Indians to sign a peace treaty with the U.S., that's all. Once in a while there's a slight legal flare-up, when some Florida county tries to force an Indian kid to go to school when he doesn't want to go—although a lot of Indians go to school now voluntarily. But there hasn't been an incident with shots fired for many years. The Seminoles have learned that they're better off than other Indian nations, in a legal way, by not signing a treaty."

"Yes." He nodded. "I learned this from M. Cassidy, but I wrote some letters first to be certain." He pursed his lips solemnly and looked down at the countertop. "I will die in Florida now. This much I know, and a Frenchman does not find it so easy to leave France when he knows he will never see it again. There are other countries in the world that would have welcomed me, M. Figueras. Greece, Italy. The world is too good to me. I have always had many good friends, friends that I have never met. They write me letters, very nice letters from all over the world."

I nodded my understanding. It was perfectly natural for strangers in every country to write to Debierue, although it had never occurred to me to write him myself. The same thing had happened to Schopenhauer in his old age, and he had been as pleased as Debierue to receive the letters. Any truly radical artist with original ideas who lives long enough will not only be accepted by the world at large, he will be admired, if not revered, for his dogged persistence—even by people who detest everything he stands for.

But there was a major difference between the old German philosopher and this old French painter. Schopenhauer had accepted the flood of congratulations on his birthdays during his seventies as a well-deserved tribute, as a vindication. Debierue, on the other hand, while grateful, seemed bewildered and even humbled by the letters he received.

"But I am not sorry I came to Florida, M. Figueras. Your sun is good for me."

"And your work? Has it gone well for you, too?"

"The artist"—he looked into my eyes—"can work anywhere. Is it not so?"

I cleared my throat to make the pitch I had been putting off. "M. Debierue, I respect your stand on art and privacy very much. In fact, just to sit here talking to you and drinking your fresh orange juice—"

"The fresh *frozen*," he emended.

". . . is an honor. A great honor. I'm well aware of your reluctance to show your work to the public and to critics, and I can't say that I blame you. You have, however, on occasion, permitted a few outstanding critics to examine and write about your work. You've only been in Florida for a few months, as I understand it, and I don't know if you've completed any paintings you'd be willing to show an American critic. But if you have, I would consider it a privilege—"

"Are you a painter, M. Figueras?"

"No, sir, I'm not. I had enough studio courses in college to know that I could never be a successful painter. My talent, such as it is, is writing, and I'm a craftsman rather than an artist, I regret to say. But I am truly a superior craftsman as a critic. To be frank, in addition to the personal pleasure I'd get from seeing your American paintings, an exclusive, in-depth article in my magazine would be a feather in my cap. The sales of the magazine would jump, and it would be the beginning for me of some very lucrative outside assignments from other art journals. As you know, only *one* photograph of any single one of your paintings would be art news big enough to get both of us international attention—"

"Do you sculpt? Or work with collage, ceramics?"

"No, sir." I tried to keep the annoyance I felt out of my voice. "Nothing like that. I'm quite inept when it comes to doing work with my hands."

"But I do not understand, M. Figueras. Your critical articles are very sensitive. I do not understand why you do not paint, or—"

"At one time this was a rather sore point with me, but I got over it. I tried hard enough, but I simply couldn't draw well enough—too clumsy, I guess. If I didn't have a well-developed verbal sense I'd prob-ably have a tough time making a living."

"I've got to go to the restroom, Mr. Debierue," Berenice said shyly.

"Certainly." Debierue came around the bar and pointed down the hallway. "The door at the far end."

I climbed off the stool when she did and looked down the hall-way past Debierue's shoulder. Berenice was undoubtedly bored, but she also undoubtedly had to go to the can. At the end of the short hallway there were two more doors *en face,* in addition to the door to the bathroom straight ahead. One door was padlocked, and one was not. The padlocked door, with its heavy hasp, was probably Debierue's studio and formerly the master bedroom of the original owner.

I took the Polaroid camera out of its leather case, and checked to see if there was an unused flash bulb in the bounce reflector.

"This camera," I said, "is so simple to operate that an eight-year-old child can get good results with it almost every time. It's that simple." I laughed. "But before I learned how to work the damned thing I ruined ten rolls of film. It's ridiculous, I know. And with typing, which I had to learn, I was equally clumsy. I took a typing course twice, but the touch system was too much for me to master." I held up my index and second fingers. "I have to type my stuff with these four fingers. So you can see why I quit trying to paint. It was too frustrating, so I quit trying before I suffered any emotional damage."

He looked at me quizzically, and stroked his hooked nose with a long finger.

"I guess I sound a little stupid," I said apologetically.

"No, no. The critic—all critics—arouses my curiosity, M. Figueras."

"It's quite simple, really. I'm purported to be an expert, or at least an authority, on art and the preschool child. And what it boils down to is this. Most motor activity is learned before the age of five. A preschool child can only learn things by doing them. And if you have a mother who does everything for you—little things like tying shoelaces, brushing your teeth, feeding you, and so on, you don't do them yourself. After five or six, when you *have* to do them yourself, in school, for example, it's too late ever to master the dexterity and motor control a painter will need in later years. Overly solicitous mothers, that is, mothers who wait on their children hand and foot, inadvertently destroy incipient artists."

"Have you ever written about this theory?"

I nodded. "Yes. A short book entitled *Art and the Preschool Child,* and I'll mail you a copy. It explains, in part, why men who are psychologically suited to becoming painters turn out so much bad art. It isn't a theory, though, it's a fact. A neglected point that I made is that such people are not lost to the world as artists. If their problem is recognized, they can be rechanneled into other artistic activities that do not call for great manual dexterity."

"Like what?" Debierue appeared to be genuinely interested.

"Writing poetry, composing electronic music. Or even architecture. The late Addison Mizner, who couldn't draw a straight line in the sand with a pointed stick, became an important South Florida architect. His buildings in Palm Beach—those that remain—are beautifully designed, and his influence on other Florida architecture has been considerable, especially here on the east coast."

I stopped before I got wound up. Debierue was pulling on me— on *me!*—one of the oldest tricks not in the book, and here I was, falling for it, just like the rawest of cub reporters. It is a simple matter for the person who is wise with the experience of being interviewed to learn the interests of the interviewer. Then, all he has to do is to keep feeding questions to the interviewer and the interviewer will end up with an interview of himself! Naively happy with a long and pleasant conversation, the interviewer will leave the subject in a blithe mood, only to learn later, when he sits chagrined at his typewriter, that he has nothing to write about.

The toilet flushed. Debierue waited politely for me to continue, but I swirled the juice in my glass, sipped the rest of it slowly until Berenice rejoined us, and then excused myself on the pretense that I also had to use the facility.

I still carried my camera, of course, and I quickly opened the door on the left of the hall, across from the padlocked door. I closed it softly behind me and took the room in rapidly. If one of Debierue's paintings was on the wall, I was going to take a picture of it. But there was only one painting on the wall, a dime-store print in a cheap black frame of *Trail's End*—the ancient Indian sitting on his wornout horse. In the 1930s almost every lower middle class home in America contained a print of *Trail's End*, but I hadn't expected to find one in Debierue's bedroom. Either Cassidy, in his meanness, had hung it on the wall, or it had been left there by the owner of the house. But I still couldn't fathom how Debierue could tolerate the corny picture, unless, perhaps, he was amused by the ironic idea behind the print. Of course, that was probably the reason.

The bedroom was austere. A Hollywood single bed, made up with apple-green sheets—and no bedspread—an unpainted pine highboy, a wrought-iron bedside table with a slab of white tile for a top, and a red plastic Charles Eames chair beside the bed made up the inventory. There was a ceiling light, but no lamp. Debierue was a nihilist and stoic in his everyday life as well as in his art, but I felt a wave of sympathy for the painter all the same. It was a shame, I felt, that this great man had so few creature comforts in his old age. There was no need for me to slide open the closet door, or to search the drawers of the highboy and paw through his clothing.

I took a nervous leak in the bathroom, and turned on the tap to wash my hands in the washbowl. I opened the mirrored cabinet to see what kind of medicines he kept there. If he had any diseases, or an illness of some kind, the medicines he used would furnish a valid clue, and that might be worth writing about. Except for Elixophyllin-K1 (an expectorant that eases the ability to breathe for persons with asthma, emphysema, and bronchitis) and three bars of Emulave (a kind of "soapless" soap, or cleansing bar for people with very dry skin—and I had noted the dryness of the painter's hands already), there was nothing out of the ordinary in the cabinet. A pearl-handled straight razor, a cup with shaving soap and brush, a bottle of blue green Scope, a half-used tube of Stripe toothpaste, a green plastic Dr. West toothbrush, a

100-tablet bottle of Bayer aspirin, with the cotton gone, and that was it. There wasn't even a comb, although Debierue, with a bald head as slick as a peeled almond, didn't need a comb. As bathroom medicine chests in America go, this was the barest cabinet—outside of a rented motel room—I had ever seen.

I returned to the living room in time to hear Berenice say, "Don't you get lonely, Mr. Debierue, living way out here all alone?"

He smiled, patted her hand, and shook his head.

"It's the nature of the artist to be lonely," I answered for him. "But the painter has his work to do, which is ample compensation."

"I know," Berenice said, "but this place is a million miles from nowhere. You ought to get a car, Mr. Debierue. Then you could drive over to Dania for jai-alai at night or something."

"No, no," he protested, still patting her hand, "I am too old now to learn how to drive an automobile."

"You could take some students," Berenice said eagerly. "There would be a lot of students who would like to work with you in your studio! And I bet they'd come with cars from all over"—she turned to me—"wouldn't they, James?"

Debierue laughed, and I joined him, although I was laughing more at Berenice's droll expression—half anger and half bewilderment— because we were laughing at her. For any other painter of equal stature, Picasso, for instance, the suggestion of a student working with a master was valid enough. But for Debierue, who showed his work to no one, the idea was absurd. Debierue had sidetracked me neatly. It was time to get back to business.

I put an affectionate arm around Berenice's waist and squeezed her as a signal to keep quiet. "You didn't answer my question a while ago, M. Debierue," I said soberly. "You have been very nice to me—to us both—even though we've invaded your privacy. But I would like to see your present work—"

He sighed. "I'm sorry, M. Figueras. You have made your visit without reason. You see," he shrugged, "I have no work to show you."

"Nothing at all? Not even a drawing?"

The corners of his mouth drooped morosely. "Work I have, yes. But what things I have done in Florida are not deserving of your attention."

"Why don't you let me be the judge of that?"

His strained half-smile was weary, but his features stiffened with a mask of discernible dignity. His voice dropped to a husky whisper. "The artist alone is the final judge of his work, M. Figueras."

I flushed. "Please don't misunderstand me," I said quickly. "I didn't mean what I said to come out that way. What I meant was that I don't intend to criticize your work, or judge it in any way. I meant to say that I would prefer to be the judge of whether I'd like to *see* it or not. And I would. It would be an honor."

"No. I am sorry but I must refuse. You are a critic and you cannot help yourself. For you, to see a picture is to make a judgment. I do not want your judgment. I paint for Debierue. I please myself and I displease myself. For a young man like you to say to me, 'Ah, M. Debierue, here in this corner a touch of terracotta might strengthen the visual weight,' or 'I like the tactile texture, but I believe I see a hole in the overall composition. . . .' " He chuckled drily. "I must say No, M. Figueras."

"You are putting me down, sir," I said. "I know there are critics such as you describe, but I'm not one of them." My face was flaming, but my voice was under control.

"With the art of Debierue, one man is a crowd. Me. Debierue. Two people are a noisy audience. But to have one spectator with a pen, the critic, is to have many thousands of spectators. Surrealism does not need your rationale, M. Figueras. And Debierue does not paint 'bicephalous centaurs.' "

"He won't let you see his pictures, will he?" Berenice guessed, looking at my face.

I shook my head.

"Maybe," she turned and looked coyly at Debierue, "you'll let me see them instead, Mr. Debierue?"

He stepped back a few feet and examined her figure admiringly. "You have a wide pelvis, my dear, and it will be very easy for you to have many fine, beautiful babies."

"By that he means No for me too, doesn't he?"

"What else?" I shrugged, and lit a cigarette.

As I had suspected, Debierue had disliked Galt's criticism. I could have begged, but that would have been abhorrent to me. If this was the way he felt there was no point in pursuing the matter anyway. In one way, he was right about me. It would have been impossible for me to look at his work without judging it. And although I would not have said anything derogatory about his work, no matter how I felt about it, there was bound to be some indication of how I felt—pro or con— reflected in my face. If he didn't actually believe that his paintings were worthy (although his faculty for criticism was certainly not as good as mine), all I could do now was take him at his word. I felt almost like crying. It was one of the greatest disappointments of my life.

"Perhaps another time, then, M. Debierue," I said.

"Yes, perhaps." He stroked his beaked nose pensively and studied my face. Not rudely, but earnestly. He glanced toward the hallway leading to his padlocked studio, looked back at me, smiled at Berenice, and tugged pensively at his lower lip. I suspect that he had expected me to put up a prolonged, involved argument, and now he didn't know whether to be grateful or disappointed by my failure to protest.

"Tell me something, M. Figueras. I am called *the* Nihilistic Surrealist, but I have never known why. Do you see much disorder here, in my little house?"

"No, sir." I looked around. "Far from it."

For an artist, the lack of clutter was most unusual. Painters, as a "class," are a messy lot. They collect things. An old board with concentric swirls, a rock with an intriguing shape, jumbles of wire, seashells, any and all kinds of things that have, to them, interesting shapes or colors. A chunk of wood, for example, may gather a heavy patina of dust for years before a sculptor finally detects the shape within the object and liberates it into a piece of sculpture.

Painters are even messier, in most instances, than sculptors. They stick drawings up here and there. Pads with sketches are scattered about haphazardly, and they clutter their quarters with all kinds of props and worthless junk. Things are needed for visual stimulation and possible ideas. This clutter is not confined to their studios either. It generally spills over into their everyday habitat, including the kitchen and bathroom.

And a Surrealist, like Debierue, dealing in the juxtaposition of the unlikely, would ordinarily require a great many unrelated objects in his home-studio to nudge his subconscious. But then, Debierue was an anomaly among painters. My experience with the habits of other painters could hardly apply to him. Besides, I had not, as yet, seen the inside of his studio. . . .

"As you see, I am an orderly, clean old man. Always it was so, even as a young man. So it may be, after all, that I am not the Surrealist. Is it not so?" The grooved amusement lines crowding his blue eyes deepened as he smiled.

"It's a relative term," I said politely. "A convenient label. 'Superrealist' or 'Subrealist' would both have served as well. The term 'Dada' itself was just a catchall word at first, but the motto 'Dada *hurts*,' when it was truly followed or lived up to in plastic expression, was quite important to me. In fact it still is, but I've always considered 'Surrealism' as a misnomer."

"Debierue does not like any label. Debierue is Debierue. Marcel Duchamp I admired very much, and he too did not like labels. Do you remember what Duchamp did when a young writer asked him for permission to write his biography?"

"No, sir."

"When Duchamp was asked for the quite personal information about himself he said nothing. He did not have to think. He emptied all of the drawers from his desk onto the floor and walked out of the room."

"An existential act." The story was one I hadn't heard.

"Another label, M. Figueras?" He clucked his tongue. "So now on the floor are odds and ends, little things saved in the desk for many years for no good reason. Snapshots, little notes one receives or makes for himself. Old letters from friends, enemies, ladies. And, what is it?—the *doodles,* little pencil squigglings. And pretty canceled stamps, saved because they are exotic perhaps. Stubs from the theater." He shrugged.

"It sounds like my desk in New York."

"But this was the Duchamp biography. The clever young man picked up everything from the floor and went away. He pasted all of the objects in a big book, entitled it *The Biography of Marcel Duchamp* and sold it for a large sum of dollars to a rich Texas Jew."

"It's funny I never heard about it. I thought I knew practically everything about Duchamp there was to know . . ."

"And so did the young man who 'wrote' the biography about Duchamp out of odds and ends from a desk."

"Nevertheless," I said, "I'd like to take a look at that book. Every scrap of information about Duchamp is important because it helps us to understand his art."

The artist shrugged. "There is no such book. The story is apocryphal—I made it up myself and spread it to a few friends many years ago to see what would happen. And because it is something Duchamp might do, many believed it as you were prepared to do. The chance debris of an artist's life does not explain the man, nor does it explain the artist's work. The true artist's vision comes from here." He tapped his forehead.

Debierue's face was expressionless now, and I was unable to tell whether he was serious, teasing me, or getting hostile. He turned to Berenice and smiled. He took her right hand in both of his and spoke in English.

"If a man had a wife and children, perhaps a short biography to leave his family, a record for them to remember him . . . but old Debierue has no wife, children, no relatives now living, to want such a book. The true artist, my dear, is too responsible to marry and have a family."

"Too responsible to fall in love?" Berenice asked softly.

"No. Love he must have."

I cleared my throat. "The entire world is the artist's family, M. Debierue. There are thousands of art lovers all over the world who would like to read your biography. Those who write to you, I know, and those who—"

He patted my arm. "Let us be the friends. It is not friendly to talk about nothing with such seriousness on your face. It is getting late, and you will both stay to dinner with me, please."

"Thank you very much. We would like very much to stay." He had changed the subject abruptly, but the longer I stayed the better my chances became to gain information about the old man. Or did they?

"Good!" He rubbed his dry hands together and they made a rasping sound. "First I will turn on my electric oven to four-two-five degrees. I do not have the printed menu, but you may decide. There is the television turkey dinner. Very good. There is the television Salisbury steak. Also very good. Or maybe, M. Figueras, you would most like the television patio dinner? Enchilada, tamale, Spanish rice, and refried beans."

"No," I said. "I guess I'll have the turkey."

"I'd rather have the Salisbury steak," Berenice said. "And let me help you—"

"No. Debierue will also have the turkey!" He smiled happily, and turned toward the stove. Relenting, he changed direction, went to the sideboard and got out a box of Piknik yellow plastic forks and spoons. There was a four-mat set of sticky rubber yellow place mats in the drawer. He handed the mats and the box of plastic utensils to Berenice and asked her to set the card table on the porch.

So far, I thought bitterly, as I glumly watched this bustling domestic activity, except for a few gossipy comments on a low curiosity level, I had picked up damned little information of any real interest from the old artist. If anything, he had learned more about me than I had about him. He had refused to let me see his work, and just as he had started to open up he had slammed the lid on what might have been an entire trunkful of fascinating material. He was a bewildering old man, all right, and I couldn't decide whether he was somewhat senile (no, not that), putting me down, with some mysterious purpose in mind, or what . . .

Working away, stripping the cardboard outer covers from the aluminum TV dinners he had taken from the freezer compartment of the purple Kentone refrigerator, Debierue sang a repetitious French song in a cracked falsetto.

No matter how he downgraded himself, false modesty or not, he was the world's outstanding Nihilistic Surrealist. That was the reason I wasn't getting anywhere with him. I was trying to talk to him as if he were a normal person. Any artist who has isolated himself from the world for three-fourths of his life either has to be a Surrealist or crazy. But Debierue was as sane as any other artist I had ever met. Even the fact that he denied being a Surrealist emphasized the fact that he was one. What else could he be? This was the rationale of the purposeful irrationality of Surrealism. The key. But the key to what?

How could a man live all alone as he did—without a phone, a TV, a radio—for months on end without going off his rocker? Even Schweitzer, when he exiled himself to Africa, took an organ along, and surrounded himself with sick, freeloading black men. . . .

From this desperate brooding, my pedestrian mind came up with one of the best original ideas I ever had, an idea so simple and direct I almost lost it. The thought was still formless, but I didn't let the idea get away from me. Berenice put three webbed chairs up to the table on the porch. She reentered the living room, and I clutched her wrist.

"I'm going to do something strange," I whispered. "But don't let on, no matter what happens. Understand?"

She nodded, and her blue eyes widened.

Debierue came out of the kitchen and tapped my wristwatch. "Sometimes I do not hear so well the timer on the oven, so you will please watch the time for us. And in thirty-five minutes when you say 'Now,' we will have the dinner all ready to eat!" He beamed his jack-o'-lantern smile at Berenice. "So simple. The television dinner is the better invention for wives than the television itself. Is it not so, my dear?"

"Oh, absolutely," Berenice said cheerfully.

"Look, M. Debierue," I said, taking my Polaroid from the bar, "I know it's a lot to ask, at least from your viewpoint, but I've got this Polaroid here, and you can see the results for yourself in about ten seconds. While we wait for dinner, let me take a few shots of you, and until we get one that you think is all right, you can just tear them up. Fair enough?"

"In only ten seconds? A picture?"

"That's all. Maybe fifteen seconds inside the house here, for a little extra snap and contrast."

He frowned slightly, and fingered his white whiskers. "My beard isn't trimmed . . ."

"In a photo, it doesn't matter. No one can tell from a black-and-white picture," I promised recklessly.

He hesitated. His eyes were wary, but he was wavering. "Should I put on a necktie?"

"No, not for an informal picture," I said, before he could change his mind. Taking him by the arm, I guided him to a point in front of the coffee table. I picked up the *Miami Herald,* flipped through it to find the classified ad section, opened it and thrust the paper into his hands.

"There. Just spread the paper, and pretend to read it. You can smile if you feel like it, but you don't have to."

A trifle self-consciously, he followed my simple directions. After focusing the camera on him, and setting it for "dark," I asked him to lower his arms slightly to make certain his face and beard would be in the picture. The flag of the *Miami Herald* and *Classified* could both be read through the viewfinder. I moved forward and touched his hand.

"Now," I admonished, "please don't move or look up at me. I'll take the photo from back there."

This was the last moment to take my premeditated chance, and one chance was all I could expect to get. I forced a loud cough to cover the slight click of my Dunhill, and ignited the paper at the bottom. A moment later, six feet back, I was squinting through the viewfinder. The timing was perfect. The bounce flash bulb worked, and it was only a split second after I snapped the shutter when the flames burst through the paper on his side and he dropped it with an astonished yelp. Berenice, who had been watching with bulging eyes and with her right hand clamped over her mouth, moved forward squealing, and began to stamp on the burning paper. I helped her, and it only took us moments to crush out the flames on the terrazzo floor.

I had expected an angry reaction from Debierue, but he was merely puzzled. "Why," he asked mildly, "did you light the paper? I don't understand." He looked about bewilderedly as the charred bits of newsprint, caught by the slight breeze coming through the jalousied door, fluttered over his clean floor.

I grinned and held up a forefinger. "Wait. Give me ten seconds, and then you'll see the picture."

I was all thumbs with excitement, but I took my time, being careful as I jerked out the strip of prepared paper that started the developing process and, instead of guessing, I watched the sweep-second hand on my watch, allowing exactly twelve seconds for the developer to work.

As curious as a child, the old artist was brushing my shoulder with his as I opened the back of the camera to remove the print. When I turned the photo face up on the bar, his jarring burst of jubilant laughter startled me.

"Don't touch it!" I said sharply, sliding the print out of the reach of his clutching fingers. "I've got to coat it first." I straightened the print on the edge of the counter and then gave it eight precise sweeps with the gooey print coater. It was the best photo, absolutely the finest, that I had ever taken.

Perfectly centered, the old man wore his wise, beautiful, infectious smile. He appeared to be reading the want ads in the *Herald* as if he didn't have a care in the world. His face was purely serene, and the deeply etched lines in his face were sharp, clear-cut, and as black as India ink. He had been completely unaware of the blazing newspaper when I snapped the picture, but no one who saw the photo would ever guess that. The entire lower half of the paper blazed furiously away. No professional model could have posed knowingly with a flaming newspaper without a slight twinge of anxiety showing in his face. But the old man, with his skinny legs exposed beneath the flames, with his bland innocent face and the wonderful smile glowing through his downy white beard, appeared as relaxed as a man who had spent a restful night in a Turkish bath.

Debierue watched me coat the print, but he kept reaching for it impatiently. I guarded it with my arm so it could dry.

"Let me see," he said childishly.

"If you touch it now," I explained patiently, "it'll pick up your fingerprints and be ruined."

"Very well, M. Figueras," he said good-naturedly. "I want this photo. It's the most formidable *surréalité* I've ever seen!"

His exuberance was as great as my own. "You'll have it, all right." I said happily. "In fact, when I get back to New York, I'll send you fifty copies of the picture if you want them, and a copy to every friend on your mailing list."

3

WHEN DEBIERUE GRANTED his permission for me to keep and publish the photograph, I hurried out to the car and got one of our magazine's standard release forms out of the glove compartment. The mimeographed form (large circulation magazines have them printed) is a simple agreement between subject and magazine to make publication legal, to protect one party from the other. There is nothing underhanded about a signed photo release. Debierue could read English, of course, but the involved legalese the form was couched in forced me to explain the damned thing at some length before he would sign it. Debierue wasn't stupid or willful. He believed naively that his oral okay was enough.

Because of this discussion, the dinners were ready before we knew it. I forgot to look at my watch, and it was Berenice who heard and recognized the faint buzzing in the kitchen as the oven timer.

It was almost pleasant on the screened porch. A light breeze came up, and although the wind was hot, it was relatively comfortable in the darkening twilight as we sat at the candlelit card table to eat the miserable off-brand TV dinners.

The dinners had been purchased by the Negro maid who came every Wednesday to take care of the old man's laundry and to do his difficult cleaning. She also brought his other weekly food supplies. By buying these cheap TV dinners, she was probably knocking down on the food money. I didn't suggest this to him, but I discussed brand names, the brand-name fallacy, and wrote out a short list of worthwhile frozen food buys he could depend upon. He had a delusion that frozen foods were better, somehow, than fresh. Berenice started halfheartedly to tell him otherwise, but when she saw me shake my head she changed the subject to domestic wines. Debierue distrusted California wines, but I added the brands of some Napa Valley wines to the frozen food list, and he said he would try them. Other than tap water, all he drank, because French wines were too dear, was frozen orange juice.

The Gold Coast for some twenty miles inland, from Jupiter downstate to Key Largo, is tropical—not *sub*tropical, as so many people erroneously believe. The tropical weather is caused by the warmth of the Gulf Stream, less than six miles off the coast. There is little difference between the weather in Miami and that of Saigon. Debierue's house, on a hammock, with a black swamp and the Everglades for a backyard, was depressingly humid. After eating the dry turkey dinner, my mouth felt as if it were dehydrated, and I couldn't drink enough fluid to unparch my throat. I poured another glass of orange juice (my fourth) and sensed, as I did so, a certain anxiety or impatience developing in the old man. As an experienced dinner guest, I have picked up an instinct about wearing out welcomes.

The sky had darkened from bruise blue to gentian violet, and it was only a few minutes after six thirty. It was much too early for him to go to bed, but even Berenice, who was not particularly observant, became aware of the old painter's restlessness. She winked across the table, tapped her wrist significantly, and gave me a brief, comical shrug. I nodded, and slid my chair back from the table.

"It's been delightful, M. Debierue, the dinner by candlelight," I lied socially, "but I have another appointment in Palm Beach tonight, and we have to drive back."

"Of course," he replied, standing, "but please keep your seat a few moments more. Already, you see, it is past the time for me to get ready. I must go to the movies tonight. I must go to the movies every night," he added, by way of fuller explanation, "and I must now change my clothes."

"The movies?" I asked stupidly.

His face brightened and he rubbed his hands together briskly. "Oh, yes, perhaps you did not see it—the Dixie Drive-in Movie Theater . . ." He pointed in the general direction of the drive-in. "Tonight there are three long features, two films with the Bowery Boys and the film about a werewolf. And before these, the regular films, there are always two and sometimes three cartoons. The first long film tonight is *The Bowery Boys Meet Frankenstein,* a very special treat, no? And if you will kindly drive me—"

"Certainly," I said eagerly, "I'll be happy to take you in the car."

"My ignorance," Debierue chuckled reminiscently, "it was the amusing thing. When I was first here and taking a walk one evening, I saw the automobiles driving inside the Dixie Drive-in Theater. I did not then know the American custom, and I thought that one must have the automobile to enter the movie. Never before had I seen the drive-in movies, and I said to myself, Why not see if the permission to go from the manager can be arranged?" So I talked then to the manager, M. Albert Price. He arranged for me to go, and gave me the Senior Citizen Golden Years' membership card." Debierue fumbled his wallet out of his hip pocket, extracted the card, which entitled him to a 15 percent discount on movie tickets, and proudly showed it to us. It was made out to Eugene V. Debs.

"That's very nice," Berenice said, smiling.

"M. Price is a very nice man," Debierue said, carefully replacing the card in his thin, calfskin wallet. "There are very good seats in front of the snack bar. The parents with the automobiles sometimes send their children to sit in these seats, and they are also for those patrons who do not have the automobile, as M. Price explained to me. Over to the right of these seats is the zinc slide and little swings, the Kiddyland for these, the children, who become tired of watching the movie screen. I *like* the children—I am a Frenchman—but the little children begin to make too much noise playing in the Kiddyland after the cartoons are finished. This arrangement is good for the parents inside the cars with speakers, but not for me. The noise becomes too loud for me. M. Price and I are now good friends, and he reserves for me each night a seat and special earphones. I hear only the movie with the earphones and no more the children."

I smiled. "Can you understand American English, the way the Bowery Boys speak it?"

"No, not always," he replied seriously. "But it is no matter. These Bowery Boys are too wonderful comedians—the Surrealist actors, no? I like M. Huntz Hall. He is very droll. Last week there were the three pictures one night with the bourgeois couple and their new house, Papa and Mama Kettle. I like them very much, and also John Wayne." He shook his fingers as if he had burned them badly on a hot stove. "Oh ho! *He* is the tough guy, no?"

"Yes, sir, he certainly is. But you've surprised me again, M. Debierue. I had no idea you were a movie fan."

"It is pleasant to see the cinema in the evenings." He shrugged. "And I like also the grape snow cone. Do you like these, the grape snow cones, M. Figueras?"

"I haven't had one in a long time."

"Very good. Fifteen cents at the snack bar."

"That's quite a long walk down there and back every night, M. Debierue. And as long as you haven't seen these old movies anyway, why don't you buy a television? There are at least a half-dozen films on TV every night, and—"

"No," he said loyally, "this is not good advice. M. Price has already explained to me that the TV was harmful to the eyes. The little screen, he said, will give one bad headaches after one or two hours of watching."

I was going to refute this, but changed my mind and lit a cigarette instead. Debierue excused himself and left for his bedroom. I stubbed out the cigarette in the sticky remains of the imitation cranberry sauce well in the TV dinner plate. My mouth was too dry to smoke.

"Have you got any tranquilizers in your purse?"

"No, but I've got a Ritalin, I think." Berenice untied the drawstring and searched for her pillbox.

"O.K., and give me two Excedrins while you're at it."

"I've only got Bufferin—"

I took two Bufferin and the tiny Ritalin pill and chased them with the remainder of my orange juice.

"It looks as though things are going to break for us after all," I said softly.

"What do you mean?"

"What do you think I mean?"

She looked at me with the blank vacant stare that always infuriated me. "I don't know."

"Never mind. We'll talk about it later."

Within a few minutes Debierue returned, wearing his moviegoer's "costume." He had exchanged the short-sleeved polo shirt for a long-sleeved dress shirt, and it was buttoned at the neck and cuffs. He wore long white duck trousers instead of shorts, and had pulled his white socks up over the cuffs and secured them with bicycle clips. With his tennis shoes and Navy blue beret he resembled some exclusive tennis club's oldest living member. In his left hand he carried a pair of cotton Iron Boy work gloves. It was a peculiar getup, but it was a practical uniform for a man who was determined to sit for six hours in a mosquito-infested drive-in movie.

Debierue locked the front door and dropped the key into a red pottery pot containing a thirsty azalea, and trailed us to the car. Berenice sat in the middle, and as I drove cautiously down the grassy road toward the highway she and the old man discussed mosquitoes and mosquito control. His beloved M. Price had a huge smoke-spraying machine on a truck that made the circuit of the theater before the films began and again at intermission, but Debierue had to take the gloves along because the mosquitoes were so fierce on his walk home. She told him about, and recommended, a spray repellent called Festrol, and I was repelled by the banality of their conversation. But with his mind on the movies, it was too late for me to ask him any final questions about his art.

I pulled over in the driveway short of the ticket window and waved a car by. I gave the old man one of my business cards with the magazine's New York address and telephone number, and wedged in a parting comment that if he changed his mind about letting me see his pictures he could call me collect at any time. He nodded impatiently and, without looking at the card, dropped it into his shirt pocket. We shook hands, the quick one-up-and-one-down handshake, Berenice gave him a peck on his beard, and he got out of the car. By the time I got the car turned around, he had disappeared into the darkness of the theater. Music and insane woodpecker laughter filled the night suddenly as I turned onto the highway. Berenice sighed.

"What's the matter?"

"Oh, I was just thinking," she said. "We held him up too long and now he'll have to wait until intermission to get his grape snow cone."

"Yeah. That's tough."

4

DROVE INTO DEBIERUE'S private road, stopped, and switched off the headlights. Before she could say anything I turned to Berenice and said, "Before you say anything I'm going to tell you. Then, if you have questions, ask them. I'm going down now to take a look at Debierue's pictures. He said he had painted a few, and now that I know there are pictures in his studio I can't go back without one for Mr. Cassidy."

"Why not? He doesn't know that there are any."

"I made a deal. And even if I decide not to take one back, which I doubt, I still have to see them myself. If you don't understand that, you don't understand me very well."

"I understand, but it's dangerous—"

"With Debierue in the movies, it's safer than houses. He dropped the door key into a potted plant on the porch. You saw him, too, didn't you?"

"But the studio is still locked, and—"

"I don't want to get you involved any more than you are already. But I want you to stay here by the highway, just in case. Debierue might think about the key himself and come back for it. I don't believe he will, but if he does you can run down the road and warn me and we'll get the hell out. Okay?"

"I can't stand out here in the dark all by myself! I'm scared and there are all these mosquitoes and I want to go with you!"

"We're wasting time. It's one thing for me to be a house-breaker, but it's something else for you—as a schoolteacher. There's nothing to be frightened about—I'm sorry about the mosquitoes—but if you're really afraid I'll take you down the highway to a gas station. You can lock yourself in the women's room till I come back for you."

"I don't want to lock myself up in—"

"Get out of the car. I want to get this over with."

"Let me have your cigarettes."

I handed her my half-empty pack, not the full one, and she climbed resignedly out of the car. "How long are you going to be?"

"I don't know. That depends upon how many paintings I have to look at."

"Don't do it, James. Please don't do it!"

"Why, for God's sake?"

"Because Debierue doesn't want you to, that's why!"

"That's not a reason."

"I—I may not be here when you get back, James."

"Good! In that case, I can say you weren't with me at all tonight if I'm caught and you won't get into any trouble."

Without lights I eased the car down the road, but turned them on again as soon as I was well into the pines and around the first bend. There was no good reason not to have taken Berenice with me except that I didn't want her along. That is, there was no rational reason. She had looked rather pitiful standing in the tall grass beside the road. Maybe I thought she would be in the way, or that she would talk all the time. Something. . . . It might have been something in my subconscious mind warning me about what I would find. As soon as I parked in front of the house I considered, for a brief moment, going back for her. I got out of the car instead, but left the headlights on.

Because of the rain-washed air the few visible stars seemed to be light years higher in the void than they usually were. There was no moon as yet, and the night was inky. In the black swamp beyond the house a lonesome bull alligator roared erotically. This was such a miserable, isolated location for an artist to live, I was grateful that the old painter had a place to go every night—and not only because the house was so easy to break into. If I had to live out here all alone, I too would have been looking forward to seeing the Bowery Boys and three color cartoons.

Debierue's "hiding" of the key was evidently a habitual practice, a safeguard to prevent its loss as he walked to and from the theater each night. I doubted that the idea entered his head that I would return to his empty house to make an illegal use of the key. But I didn't really know. My guilt, if any, was light. I felt no more guilt than that of a professional burglar. A burglar must make a living, and to steal he must first invade the locked home where the items he wants to steal are safeguarded. I meant no harm to the old artist. Any picture I took, and I was only going to take one, Debierue could paint again. And except for the visual impressions of his paintings in my mind—and a few photos—I would take nothing else. There was no reason to feel guilty.

So I cannot account for the dryness of my mouth, the dull stasis of my blood, the tightness of the muscles surrounding my stomach, and the noticeable increase in my rate of breathing. These signs of anxiety were ridiculous. The old man was sitting in the drive-in with a pair of headphones clamped to his ears, and even if he caught me inside the house, the worst he could do would be to express dismay. He couldn't hurt me physically, and he would hardly report me to the police. But I was an amateur. I had never broken into anyone's house before, so I supposed that my anxiety stemmed from the melodramatic idea that I was engaged in a romantic adventure. But after I had unlocked the front door and let it swing inward, I had to muster a good deal of courage before I could force my hand to reach inside to flip on the living room lights.

The light coming through the window would be bright enough to see my way back from the car. I switched off the headlights, and returned hurriedly to the house with a tire iron and a hammer I got from the trunk. But as it turned out, these tools were unnecessary.

The only barrier to the studio was the hasp and the heavy Yale lock on the door. Once broken there would be no way to prevent Debierue from guessing that I had returned. But if the artist had been afraid he might lose his house key, it also seemed unlikely that he would take the studio padlock key to the theater.

Switching on the lights as I searched, I made a hasty, fruitless examination of the kitchen before moving on to the bedroom. Two keys together on a short twist of copper wire, both of them identical, were in plain view on top of the highboy dresser. I unlocked the padlock, opened the studio door, and flipped the row of toggles on the wall. The boxlike windowless room, after hesitant blue-white flickers, brightened into an icy, intense brilliance. There were a dozen overhead fluorescent tubes in parallel sets of three (two blue white to one yellow) flush with the ceiling. Under this cold light I noticed first the patching of new brickwork that filled the spaces where two windows had been before, despite the new coat of white enamel that covered the walls.

Blinking my eyes to accustom them to the intense overhead light, I closed the door behind me. My thumping heart was prepared for the impact of the unusual, the unique, for the miraculous in visual art, but instead of wine and fish I didn't find even bread and water.

There were canvases, at least two dozen of them, and all of these pristine canvases were the same size, 24" x 30". They were stacked in white plastic racks against the western wall. The racks were the commercial kind one often finds in art supply stores. I checked every one of these glittering white canvases. None of them had been touched by paint or charcoal.

There was a new, gunmetal desk in the southwest corner of the studio, with a matching chair cushioned in light gray Naugahyde. On the desk there was a fruit jar filled with sharpened pencils and ballpoint pens, a square glass paperweight (slightly magnified) holding down some correspondence, and a beautiful desk calendar (an Almanacco Artistico Italiano product in brilliant colors, made by Alfieri & Lacroix, Milano). Without shame, I read the two letters that had been held down by the paperweight. One was a letter from a Parisian clipping service, stating that Debierue's name had been mentioned twice in the foreword to a new art history pictorial collection, but inasmuch as the illustrated volume was quite expensive, the manager had written to the publisher and requested a courtesy copy for Debierue. He would send it along as soon as—or if—he received it. There was a news clipping from *Paris Soir,* an unsigned review of a Man Ray retrospective exhibit in Paris, and Debierue's name was mentioned, together with the names of a dozen other artists, in a listing of Dadaists who had known Man Ray during the 1920s.

Debierue had answered the manager of the clipping service in a crabbed, backhanded script with cursive letters so microscopic he must have written the letter with the aid of the magnified paperweight. He merely told the manager not to send the book if he got a free copy, and not to buy it if he did not. Except for Debierue's surname (the tiny lowercase letters "e" through "e" were all contained within a large capital "D") there was no complimentary closing. Debierue had a unique signature. I folded the letter and put it into the breast pocket of my jumpsuit.

As I looked through the unlocked drawers of the desk, I found nothing else to hold my interest, except for a scrapbook of clippings. The scrapbook, 10" x 12", bound in gray cardboard covers, was less than half filled, and from the first clipping to the last one pasted in, covered an eighteen-month period. Most of the earlier clippings were reports of the fire that had burned down his villa, similar accounts from many different newspapers. The more recent clippings were shorter—like the mention of his name in the Man Ray art review. The items in the other drawers were what one expects to find. Stationery and supplies, stamps, glue, correspondence in manila folders— unusual perhaps because of the meticulous neatness one doesn't associate with desk drawers.

There was a two-shelf, imitation walnut bookcase beside the desk that held about thirty books. Most of them were paperbacks, five *policiers* from the *Série Noire,* three Simenons and two by Chester Himes, Pascal's *Pensées, From Caligari to Hitler, Godard on Godard,* an autographed copy of Samuel Beckett's *Proust,* and several paperback novels by French authors I had never heard of before. The hardcover books were all well worn. A French-English dictionary and a French-German dictionary, in library reference size, a tattered copy of *Heidi* (in German), a boxed two-volume edition of Schopenhauer's *The World as Will and Idea* (also in German), *Les Fleurs du Mal,* and an autographed copy of August Hauptmann's *Debierue.* I fought down my impulse to steal the autographed copy of Beckett's *Proust,* the only book in the small library I coveted, and scribbled the list of book titles into my notebook.

In addition to the books, there were several neat piles of art magazines, including *Fine Arts: The Americas,* all of them in chronological order, with the most recent issues on the top of each stack, arranged along the wall. I considered leafing through these magazines to look for drawings, but it would be absurd for Debierue, with his keen sense of order, to hide sketches in magazines.

In the center of the studio was a maple worktable (in furniture catalogues, they are called "Early American Harvest" tables), and this table, in a rather finicky arrangement, held a terracotta jar with several new camel's-hair brushes in varying lengths and brush widths, four rubber-banded, faggoty bundles of charcoal drawing sticks, four one-quart cans of linseed oil and four one-quart cans of turpentine, all unopened, and a long row of king-sized tubes of oil paint in almost every shade and tint on the spectrum.

There were at least a hundred tubes of oil paint, in colors, and three of zinc white. None of the tubes had been opened or squeezed. There was a square piece of clear glass, about 12" x 12", a fumed oak artist's palette, a pair of white gloves (size 9½), a twelve-inch brass ruler, a palette knife, an unopened box of assorted color pencils, and a heaped flat pile of clean white rags. There were other unused art materials as well, but the crushing impression of this neatly ordered table was that of a commercial layout of art materials in an art supply showroom.

Beside the table was an unpainted wooden A-frame easel and a tall metal kitchen stool painted in white enamel. There was an untouched 24" x 30" canvas on the easel. Bewildered, and with a feeling of nausea in the pit of my stomach, I climbed onto the high stool facing the easel and lit a cigarette. A single silver filament, a spider's let-down thread, shimmering in the brilliant light washing the room from the overhead fluorescents, trailed from the right-hand corner of the canvas to the floor. The spider who had left this evidence of passage had disappeared.

Except for the pole-axed numbness of a steer, my mind was too stunned for a contiguous reaction of any kind. I neither laughed nor cried. For minutes I was unable to formulate any coherent thoughts, not until the cigarette burned my fingers, and even then I remember looking at it stupidly for a second or so before dropping it to the floor.

Debierue's aseptically forlorn studio is as clear in my mind now as if I were still sitting on that hard metal stool.

I had expected something, but not Nothing.

I had expected almost anything, but not Nothing.

Prepared for attendance and appreciation, my mind could not undo its readiness for perception and accept the unfulfilled *preparation* for painting it encountered.

Here was a qualified Nothing, a Nothing of such deep despair, I could not be absolved of my aesthetic responsibility—a nonhope Nothing, a non-Nothing—and yet, also before my eyes was the evidence of a dedication to artistic expression so unyieldingly vast in its implications that my mind—at least at first—bluntly refused to accept the evidence.

I had to work it out.

The synecdochic relationship between the place and the person was undeniable. An artist has a studio: Debierue had a studio: Debierue was an artist.

Here, in deadly readiness, Debierue sat daily in fruitless preparation for a painting that he would never paint, waiting for pictorial adventures that would never happen. *Waiting,* the incredibly patient waiting for an idea to materialize, for a single idea that could be transferred onto the ready canvas—but no ideas ever came to him. Never.

Debierue worked four hours a day, he claimed, which meant sitting on this stool staring at an empty canvas from eight until noon, every day, seven days a week, waiting for an idea to come—every single day! At that precise moment I *knew,* despite all of the published documentary evidence to the contrary, that he was not merely suffering a so-called dry period, a temporary inability to paint since moving to Florida. Without any other evidence (my own eyes were witness enough, together with my practiced critical intuition), I *knew* that Jacques Debierue had never had a plastic idea, nor had he painted a picture of any kind in his entire lifetime!

Debierue was a slave to hope. He had never accepted the fact that he couldn't paint a picture. But each day he faced the slavery of the attempt to paint, and the subsequent daily failure. After each day of failure he was destroyed, only to be reborn on the next day—each new day bringing with it a new chance, a new opportunity. How could he be so strong willed to face this daily death, this vain slavery to hope? He had dedicated his life to Nothing.

The most primitive nescience in man cannot remain completely negative—or so I had always believed. Forms and the spectrum range of colors, the sounds a man makes with his mouth, the thousands of daily perceptions of sights and sound, invade our senses from moment to moment, consciously and subconsciously. And all of these sights and sounds—and touch, too, of course—demand an artistic interpretation. Knowing this basic natural truth, I knew that Debierue, an intelligent, sentient human being, must have had hundreds, no, literally thousands of ideas for paintings during the innumerable years he sat before an empty canvas. But these ideas were unexpressed, locked inside his head, withheld from graphic presentation because of his fear of releasing them. He was afraid to take a chance, he was unable to risk the possibility—a distinct possibility—of failure. His dread of failure was not a concern with what others might think of his work. It was a fear of what he, Debierue, the Artist, might think of his accomplished work. The moment an artist expresses himself and fails, or commits himself to an act of self-expression by action, and realizes that he did not, that he cannot, succeed, and that he will never be able to capture on canvas that which he sees so vividly in his mind's eye, he will know irrevocably that he is a failure as an artist.

So why should he paint? In fact, how can he paint?

How many times had Debierue leaned forward, reaching out timidly toward the shining canvas before him with a crumbling piece of charcoal in his trembling fingers? How many times?—and with the finished, varnished, luminous masterpiece glowing upon the museum wall of his febrile mind?—only to stay his hand at the last possible moment, the tip of the black charcoal a fraction of an inch away from the virgin canvas?

"Nonono! Not yet!"

The fear-crazed neural message would race down the full length of the motor neuron in his extended arm (vaulting synapse junctions), and in time, always in the nick of time, the quavery hand would be jerked back. The virgin canvas, safe for another day, would once again remain unviolated.

Another day, another morning of uncommitted, untested accomplishment had been hurdled, but what difference did it make? What did anything matter, at high noon, so long as he had delayed, put off until tomorrow, postponed the execution of the feeble idea he had today when there would be a much better idea tomorrow? If he did not prove to himself today that he could paint the image in his mind, or that he could *not* paint it, a tendril of comfort remained. And hope.

Faith in his untried skills provided a continuum.

Why not? Wasn't he trying? Yes. Was he not a dedicated artist? Yes. Did he ever fail to put in his scheduled work period every day? No. Was he not faithful to the sustained effort?—the devoted, painful, mental concentration?—the agony of creation? Yes, yes, and yes again.

And who knew? Who knows? The day might arrive soon, perhaps tomorrow! that bright day when an idea for a painting would come to him that was so powerful, so tremendous in scope and conception, that his paint-loaded brush could no longer be withheld from the canvas! He would strike at last, and a pictorial masterpiece would be born, delivered, created, a painting that would live forever in the hearts of men!

All through life we protect ourselves from countless hurtful truths by being a little blind here—by ignoring the something trying to flag

our attention on the outer edges of our peripheral vision, by being
a little shortsighted there—by being a trifle too quick to accept the
easiest answer, and by squinting our eyes against the bright, incoming
light all of the time. Emerson wrote once that even a corpse is beautiful if you shine enough light on it.

But that is horseshit.

Too much light means unbearable truth, and too much truthful
light sears a man's eyes into an unraging blindness. The blind man can
only smell the crap of his life, and the sounds in his ears are cacoph-
onous corruptions. Without vision, the terrible beauty of life is irrevocably gone. Gone!

And as I thought of all Debierue's lost visions, never to appear
on canvas for the exhilaration of my eyes, scalding tears ran down
my cheeks.

PART THREE

If Anything Was Comprehensible, It Would Be Incommunicable

1

I TOOK MY TIME.

What I had to do had to be done right or not at all. Once I committed, although my concern for Berenice (frightened and waiting for me in the tall grass by the highway) did not diminish, it would have been foolhardy to rush. I might have overlooked something important.

I looked in the kitchen for string and wrapping paper, but there was neither. There was newspaper, but it would have been awkward to wrap a canvas in newspaper when there was no string to tie the bundle. There were several large brown paper grocery sacks under the sink, and I took one of these back to the studio to hold the art materials I would need. I took a clean sheet from the hall linen closet and wrapped one of the new canvases from the plastic rack in it. I then filled the brown sack with several camel's-hair brushes, a can of turpentine, one of linseed oil, and a half-dozen tubes of oil paint. With cadmium red, chrome yellow, Prussian blue, and zinc white I can mix almost any shade or tint of color I desire (this much I had learned in my first oil painting course because the tyrannical teacher had made us learn how to mix primary colors if he taught us nothing else). I added tubes of burnt sienna and lampblack to the others because they were useful for skin tones (there were no compositional ideas in mind at the time, just nebulous multicolored swirls floating loosely about in my head) if some figures became involved in the composition. The palette knife was also useful and I dropped it into the sack, but I didn't take the expensive palette. It was too expensive and could be traced, and I wouldn't want to be caught with it in my possession.

These art materials could be purchased anywhere, of course, as could the prepared 30" x 24" canvas, but I needed Debierue's materials in the event the authenticity of the painting was ever questioned. Mr. Cassidy, who had purchased everything for Debierue, would have a bill from the art store listing these materials, their brands, and so would Rex Art. My mind was racing, but I was clearheaded enough to realize how close a scrutiny the painting would receive when and if it were ever painted and exhibited.

I put the wrapped canvas, the sackful of supplies, and the hammer and tire iron into the trunk of the car, and returned to the studio.

I ran into trouble with the fire. Turpentine is flammable, highly flammable, but I had difficulty in getting it lighted and in keeping it burning once it was lit. I finally had to take the remains of the *Miami Herald*, crumple each separate page into a ball, and partially soak each sheet with turpentine before I could get a roaring fire started beneath the Early American Harvest table.

Once it got started, however, the fire burned beautifully. I poured most of the last can on the studio door, and dribbled the rest to the blaze beneath the table. I then tossed the new canvases into the fire, and backed out of the room. Because the fire would need a draft, I left the studio door and the front door standing open. Whether the house burned down or not was unimportant. The important thing was a charred and well-gutted studio. I wanted no evidence of any paintings left behind, and the crackling prepared canvases, sized with white lead, burned rapidly.

Satisfied, I turned out the living room and kitchen lights and got into the car. When I reached the highway and stopped, Berenice was gone. I shouted her name twice and panicked momentarily. Had she hitchhiked a ride back to Palm Beach? If she stuck out her thumb, any truck driver who saw it would stop and pick her up. But I calmed down by putting myself in her place, turned toward the drive-in theater instead of turning left for Palm Beach, and found her waiting for me in the gravel road of the driveway, standing near the well-lighted marquee.

"What took you so long?" Her voice wasn't angry. She was too relieved to see me, happy to be in the car again. "I thought you were never coming back."

"I'm sorry. It took longer than I expected."

"Did you stea— take a picture?"

"Yeah."

"What were they like? The pictures?"

"I'll turn over here U.S. One. There're too many trucks on Seven."

"How long do you think it'll be, before he misses the picture?"

"I've got to go back to New York, Berenice. Tonight. So as soon as we get back to the apartment I'll pack—you're still packed, practically—and then I can drop you off at the airport. Or, if you'd rather, you can stay on for a few more days. The rent's paid till the end of the month, so . . ."

"If you're going to New York, so am I!"

"But what's the point? You've got your school year contract, and you have to go back to work, don't you? Besides, I'm going to be busy. I won't have any time for you at all. First, there's the Debierue article to write, and the deadline is tighter than hell now. I'll have to find a place to crash. The man in my pad has still got another month on the sublease, you see. I'm almost broke, and I'll have to borrow some money, and—"

"Money isn't a problem, James. I've got almost five hundred dollars in traveler's checks, and more than five thousand in savings in the credit union. I'm going to New York with you.

"Okay," I said bitterly, "but you'll have to help me drive."

"Watch out!" she shrilled. "That car's only got one headlight!"

"I don't mean *that* way. I mean to spell me at the wheel on the way up, so we can make better time."

"I know what you meant, but you might have thought it was a motorcycle. We can trade off every two hours."

"No. When I get tired, we'll trade."

"All right. How're you going to get your twenty dollars back?"

"What twenty dollars?"

"The deposit at the electric company. If we leave tonight, you won't be able to have them cut off the electricity or get your deposit back."

"Jesus, I don't know. I can let the landlady handle it and send me the money later. They'll subtract what I owe anyway. Please, Berenice, I'm trying to think. I've got so much on my mind I don't want to hear any more domestic crap, and those damned non sequiturs of yours drive me up the goddamned tree."

"I'm sorry."

"So am I. We're both sorry, but just be quiet."

"I will. I won't say anything else."

"Nothing else! Please!"

Berenice gulped, closed her generous mouth, and puckered her lips into a prim pout. She looked straight ahead through the windshield and twisted her gloves, which she had removed, in her lap. I had shouted at her, but in my agitation, somehow, had consented to take her with me to New York. This was the last thing I wanted to do. It would take two days, perhaps three, to write the article on Debierue—and I had to do something about the painting for Mr. Cassidy. It wasn't a task I could have done for me, although I knew a dozen painters in New York who could have produced anything on canvas I asked them to put there, and the product would have been a professional job.

But no one could be trusted. It was something I had to do myself, to fit Debierue's "American Period"—at that moment I coined the title for my article: "Debierue: The American Harvest Period." It was a major improvement over my previous title, and "American Harvest"—the idea must have come to me from the worktable in his studio—would provide me with a springboard for generating associative ideas.

But there was still Berenice, and the problem of what to do with her—but wasn't it better to have her with me than to simply turn her loose where she could learn about the fire by reading about it in a newspaper, or by hearing a newscast? How soon would the report go out? Would Debierue telephone Mr. Cassidy and tell him about it? That depended upon the extent of the fire, probably, but Cassidy would be the only person Debierue knew to contact, and I could certainly trust Cassidy to make the correct decision. He might inform the news media, and again he might not. Before doing anything, he would want to know whether I got a picture for him before the fire started. And although Cassidy might suspect me of setting the fire, he wouldn't know for sure, and he wouldn't give a damn about the other "paintings" destroyed in the fire so long as he got his.

I still had about three hours, or perhaps closer to four, to contact Cassidy before Debierue learned about the fire and managed to telephone him.

And Berenice? It would be best to keep her with me. At least for now. Once we reached New York, I could settle her in a hotel for a few days until I finished doing the things I had to do, and then we could work out a compromise of some kind. The best compromise, and I could work out the details later, would be for her to return to Duluth and teach until the summer vacation. In this way, "we could reflect upon how we *really* felt about each other—at a sane distance, without passion interfering—and, if we both felt as if we still loved each other, in truth, and our affair was not just a *physical* thing, well, we could then work out some kind of life arrangement together when we met in New York—or somewhere—during her two-month summer vacation."

This was an idea I could sell, I decided, but until I had time for it, she could stay with me for the ride. It would take hours of argument to get rid of her now, and I simply couldn't spare the time on polemics when I had to concentrate every faculty I possessed on Debierue, his "American Harvest" period, his painting, and what I was going to write.

I took the Lake Worth bridge to pick up A1A, to enter Palm Beach from the southern end of the island, and Berenice shifted suddenly in her seat.

"Do you know that we've driven for more than forty-five minutes, and you haven't said a single word?"

"Crack your wind-wing a little, Honey," I said, "and we'll get some more air."

"Oh!" She cracked the window. "You're the most exasperating man I've ever met in my life, and if I didn't love you so much I'd tell you so!"

By leaving the food in the refrigerator, and the canned food and staples on the shelves, it didn't take us long to pack. I put my clean clothes in my small suitcase, and the dirty clothes, which made up the bulk of my belongings, all went into the big valopack with my suits, slacks, and jackets. While Berenice looked around to see if we had forgotten anything, I took my bags and typewriter to the car and tossed them into the back seat.

On my way back for Berenice's luggage I stopped at the landlady's apartment, gave her the receipt for the power company's twenty-dollar deposit, and told her to take the money that remained to pay someone to clean the apartment. When she began to protest that this small sum wouldn't be enough to pay a cleaning woman, I told her to add the balance of the rent money I had paid her in advance instead of returning it to me and she said: "I hope you have a pleasant trip back to New York, Mr. Figueras, and perhaps you'll drop me a card some time from Spanish Harlem."

She was a real bitch, but I shrugged off her parting remark and returned to the apartment for Berenice and her things.

I stopped at the Western Union office in Riviera Beach and sent two telegrams. The first one, to my managing editor in New York, was easy:

> hold my space 5000 words personal article on
> debierue driving with it now to ny figueras

This telegram would put Tom Russell into a frenzy, but he would hold the space, or rip out something else already set for a piece on Debierue. But he would be so astonished about my having an article written on Debierue he wouldn't know whether to believe me or not. And yet, he would be afraid not to believe me. I gave the operator his home address on Long Island, and the New York magazine address as well, with instructions to telephone the message to him before delivering it. The girl assured me that he would have it before midnight, which assured me that Tom would have a sleepless night. Well, so would I.

The wire to Joseph Cassidy at the Royal Palm Towers, only a twenty-minute drive from Riviera Beach at this time of evening, was more difficult to compose. I threw away the first three drafts, and then sent the following as a night letter, with instructions not to deliver it until at least eight A.M:

> emergency stop urgent i report to ny mag-
> azine office stop will write and send picture
> from there figueras

There was ambiguity in the wording, but I wanted it to read that way. He would not be able to ascertain from the way the wire was worded whether I would write and fill him in on the "emergency," or whether I would be sending Debierue's "picture" from New York. If nothing else, the wire would make him cautious about what he would say to the press about Debierue and the fire, although I knew he would have to release something. Knowing that *he* didn't set the fire, and without knowing for sure that *I* had set it, Debierue would most certainly contact Cassidy. If he suspected that the fire had been set by vandals, Debierue would probably be afraid to stay at the isolated location even though the rest of the house was only slightly damaged.

Berenice, happy to have her way about going to New York, sat in the car while I sent the telegrams, and, except for humming or singing snatches of Rodgers & Hart songs, confined her conversation to reminding me occasionally to dim my lights or to kick them to bright again. Brooding about what to write, and how to write it, especially after we got onto the straight, mind-dulling Sunshine Parkway, I needed frequent reminders about the headlights.

The rest-stop islands, with filling stations at each end, and Dobbs House concession restaurants sandwiched between the gas stations, are staggered at uneven distances along the Parkway. Because they are unevenly spaced, it wasn't possible to stop at every other one (sometimes it was only twenty-eight miles to a rest stop, whereas the next one would be sixty miles away), and a decision, usually to halt, had to be made every time. Berenice always went to the can twice, once upon debarking, and again after we had a cup of coffee. I said nothing about the delay (as a man I could have stopped anywhere along the highway, but I would have been insane to make such a suggestion to a middle-western schoolteacher), and besides, the rest stops soon became useful. Sitting at the counter over coffee with my notebook, I organized my vagrant thoughts about Debierue's "American

Harvest" Florida paintings, and by writing down my ideas at each stop, I retained the good ones, eliminated the poor ones, and gradually developed a complicated, but pyramiding, gestalt for the article.

I allowed Berenice to drive between the Fort Pierce and Yeehaw Junction rest stops, but, finding that I thought better at the wheel, persuaded her to put her head on my shoulder and go to sleep with the promise that she could drive all the next morning while I slept. Toward morning the air became nippy, but by nine A.M., with Berenice driving, as we entered the long wide thoroughfare leading into downtown Valdosta, I knew that we had to stop.

If I didn't write the piece on Debierue now, while my ideas were still fresh, the article would suffer a hundred metamorphoses in my mind during the long haul to New York. I would be bone tired by then, confused, and unable to write anything. There were some references, dates, names, and so on, I would have to check in New York, but I could write the piece now and leave those spaces blank. Besides, Tom Russell would want to read the piece the moment I got into the city. I also had to paint a picture before I wrote the article. By looking at it (whatever it turned out to be), it would be a simple matter to describe the painting with it sitting in front of me, and I could tie the other paintings to it somehow.

"Berenice," I said, "we're going to stop here in Valdosta, not in a motel, but in the hotel downtown, if they have one. In a hotel we can get room service, and two rooms, one for you and—"

"Why two rooms? Why can't I—"

"I know you mean well, sweetheart, and you're awfully quiet when I'm working, but you also know how it bugs me to have you tiptoeing around while I'm trying to write. I won't have time to talk to you while I'm working, and I won't stop, once I start, until I've got at least a good rough draft on paper. Take a long nap, a good tub bath—motels only have showers, you know—and then go to a movie this afternoon. And tonight, if I'm fairly well along with it, we can have dinner together."

"Shouldn't you sleep for a few hours first? I had some catnaps, but you haven't closed your eyes."

"I'll take a couple of bennies. I'm afraid if I go to sleep I'll lose my ideas."

Being reasonable with Berenice worked for once. Downtown, we stopped at the tattered-awninged entrance of a six-story brick hotel, The Valdosta Arms. I asked the ancient black doorman if the hotel had a parking garage.

"Yes, sir," he said. "If you checking in, drive right aroun' the corner there and under the buildin'. I'll have a bellman waitin' there for your bags."

I reached across Berenice and handed the old man two quarters.

"If you want out here, I'll carry your car aroun' myself," he offered.

"No," I shook my head. "I like to know where my car is parked."

He was limping for the house phone beside the revolving glass doors before Berenice got the car into gear.

I wanted to know where the car was parked because I intended to return for the canvas and art materials after getting Berenice settled in. The bellman had a luggage truck waiting, and we followed him into the service elevator and up to the lobby.

"Two singles, please," I said to the desk clerk. A bored middle-aged man, his eyes didn't even light up when he looked at Berenice.

"Do you have a reservation, sir?"

"No."

"All right. I can give you connecting rooms on three, if you like."

"Fine," Berenice said.

"No." I smiled and shook my head. "You'd better separate them. I have to do some typing, and we've been driving all night and it might disturb her sleep."

"Five-ten, and Five-oh-five." He shifted his weary deadpan to address Berenice. "You'll be dreckly across the hall from him, Miss."

I signed a register card, and while Berenice was signing hers, crossed to the newsstand and looked for her favorite magazine on the rack. Unable to find it, I asked the woman behind the glass display case if she had sold out her *Cosmopolitans*. Setting her lips in a prim line, she reached beneath the counter and silently placed a copy on the glass top. I handed her a dollar and she rang it up (a man who buys "under the counter" magazines has to pay a little more). I joined Berenice and the bellman at the elevators and we went up to our rooms.

The first thing I did after tipping the bellman and closing the door was to change out of my jumpsuit. From the guarded but indignant looks I had received in the lobby from the newsstand woman, the bellman, and two blue-suited men with narrow ties (the desk clerk's face wouldn't have registered surprise if I had worn jockey shorts), gentlemen were not expected to wear jumpsuits in downtown Valdosta. And I didn't want people to stare at me when I went down to the basement garage for my art materials. I put on a pair of gray slacks, a white silk shirt, with a white-on-white brocade tie, and a lime sports jacket, the only unrumpled clothes I had.

By taking the service elevator down and up, I was back in my room in fewer than five minutes. The room was hot and close. I stripped to my underwear, turned the air-conditioner to "Cool," and put the blank canvas against the back of a straight laddered chair. There was a large, fairly flat, green ceramic ashtray on the coffee table. This ashtray served to steady the canvas upright against the back of the chair, and would perform double duty as a palette. I squeezed blobs of blue, yellow, red, and white paint onto the ashtray, opened the cans of turpentine and linseed oil, lined up the brushes on the coffee table, and stared at the canvas. After fifteen minutes, I brought the other straight-backed chair over from the desk, sat down on it, and stared at the blank canvas some more.

Twenty minutes later, still staring at the white canvas, I was shivering. I turned the reverse-cycle air-conditioner to "Heat," and fifteen minutes later I was roasting, with perspiration bursting out of my forehead and clammy streams of sweat rolling down my sides from my damp armpits. I turned off the air-conditioner and tried to raise the window. The huge air-conditioner occupied the bottom half of the window, and the top half of the window was nailed shut, with rusty red paint covering the nailheads. But there was an over-head fan, and the switch still worked. The fan, with wobbly two-foot blades, turned lazily in the high ceiling. The room was still close, so I unlocked the door, and kept it ajar with an old-fashioned brass hook-and-eye attachment that held the door cracked open approximately four inches. No one could see in from the corridor and within minutes the room was perfectly comfortable with just enough fresh air coming in from the hallway to be gently wafted about by the slow and not unpleasantly creaking overhead fan.

An hour later I was still physically comfortable. I had smoked three Kools. I was still staring at the virgin canvas, and realized, finally, that I was unable to paint an original Debierue painting. Not even if I sat there for four straight hours every day . . .

2

MY EYES, BRIGHT and alert, stared at the blank, shining canvas, and my stout heart, stepped up slightly, if inaudibly, from the depressing uppityness of two nugatory bennies, pumped willing blood to my even more willing fingers. I had forgotten, for two wasted hours, the hard-learned lesson of our times. In this, the Age of Specialization, where we can only point to Hugh Hefner or, wilder yet, to the early Marlon Brando as our contemporary "Renaissance Men," I had tackled my problem ass-backwards.

I was a writer confined by choice but still confined to contemporary art—writing about it, not painting it. I could wield a paintbrush, of course, passably. I had learned to paint in college studio courses before going on to my higher calling, in the same way that a man who wants to become a brigadier general and command an Air Force wing must first learn how to fly an airplane. The general does not have to be a superior pilot to command a wing, but he attains his position because, as an ex- or now part-time pilot, he understands the daily flight problems of the pilots under his command. The system doesn't work very well, of course, because the man who wants to fly an Air Force jet, and plans his career accordingly, seldom enters that active occupation with the preconceived plan of ending up some day at a desk where he rarely flies. The "hot" pilot does not make a good paper-shuffling general because the makeup of a man who wants to fly does not include a love of administration, writing letters, and enforcing discipline.

I had learned how to paint because I had to learn the problems confronting painters, and I had taught college students because that was what I had to do to survive as an art historian. But in my secret heart I had intended to become an art critic from the very beginning. And although my major passion was contemporary art, during my year in Europe I had grimly made my rounds in the Louvre, in Florence, in Rome, tramping dutifully through ancient galleries because I knew that I had to examine the art of the past to understand the art of the present.

I was a writer, not a painter, and a writer gets his ideas from a blank piece of paper, not from a blank piece of canvas. I moved my chair to the desk and my typewriter and immediately started to write.

This is the way it works. The contemporary painter approaches his canvas without an idea (in most cases), fools around with charcoal, experimenting with lines and forms, filling in here, using a shaping thumb, perhaps, to add some depth to a form that is beginning to interest him, and sooner or later he *sees* something. The painting develops into a composition and he completes it. His subconscious takes over, and the completed painting may turn out well or, more often than not, like most writing, turn out badly. Even when the painter begins with an idea of some kind his subconscious takes over the painting once he starts working on it. The same theory, essentially, holds true for the writer. A man paints or writes both consciously and subconsciously beginning with, at most, a few relevant mental notes.

So once I sat at my typewriter, the article began to take shape. One idea led quickly to another. It was an inspired piece of work, because it was morally right to write it. My honor and Debierue's were both at stake. And yet, although it was in some respects easy to write, it was one of the most difficult pieces I had ever written because of the fictional elements it contained.

My creative talents flagged when it came to describing the pictures Debierue had failed to paint, although, once over this block, it was a simple matter to interpret the paintings because I could visualize them perfectly in my mind's eye. I was familiar enough with Debierue's background to summarize the historical details of his earlier accomplishments. It was also simple enough to record a tightly edited version of our conversation, with a few embellishments for clarity, and a few bits of profundity for reader interest. Perhaps there is a little something of the fiction writer inside every professional journalist.

My imaginative powers were strong enough to describe the paintings that I, myself, would have liked to paint if I had had the ability to paint them, but I ran into conceptual difficulties because, at first, I thought I had to describe the paintings that *Debierue* wanted to paint. But this was a futile path. I could not possibly see the world as Debierue did. And if I was unable to live in his arcane world, I could never verbalize it into visual art.

My predetermined term, "American Harvest," for Debierue's so-called American period, provided me with the correlative link I needed to visualize mental pictures I was capable of describing. I began with red, white, and blue—the colors of France's noble tricolor and our own American flag. Seeing these three colors on three separate panels I began to rearrange the panels in my mind. Side by side, in a row, close together, well separated, overlapping, horizontal and vertical with the floor, and scattered throughout a room on three different walls. But there are four walls to a room. A fourth panel was required—not for symmetry, because that doesn't matter—but for variety, for the sake of an ordered environment. Florida. Sun. Orange. An autumnal sun for Debierue's declining years. Burnt orange. But not a panel of burnt orange in toto—that would be heresy, because

Debierue, even at his great age, was still painting, still creating, still growing. So the ragged square of burnt orange required a lustrous border of blue to surround the dying sun and to overflow the edges of the rectangle. Bluebird blue? Sky blue? No, not sky nor Dufy blue, because that meant using cobalt oil paint, and cobalt blue, with the passage of years, gradually turns to bluish gray. Prussian blue, with a haughty whisper of zinc white added to make it bitterly bold. Besides, right here in this hotel room, I had a full tube of Prussian blue.

Texture? Tactile quality? Little if any. Pure, smooth, even colors.

The four paintings, 30" x 24", were the only paintings Debierue had painted since coming to Florida. The paintings were for his personal aesthetic satisfaction, to enjoy during the harvest years of his stay in America, and yet they were in keeping with his traditionally established principles of Nihilistic Surrealism.

Every morning when Debierue arose at six A.M., depending upon his waking mood, he hung one of the red, white, or blue panels next to the permanently centered burnt orange, blue-bordered panel, the painting representing the painter—the painter's "self." For the remainder of the day, when he was not engaged in the planning of another (undisclosed to the writer) work of art, he studied and contemplated the two bilateral paintings which reminded him of America's multiple "manifest destinies," the complexities of American life in general, and his personal artistic commitment to the new world.

Did he ever awaken in a mood buoyant enough to hang two or perhaps three panels at once alongside the burnt orange panel?

"No," he said.

I had typed eighteen pages for a total of 4,347 words. Now that the concept was firmly established, I could have gone on to write another dozen pages of interpretive commentary, but I forced myself to stop with the negative. Wasn't it about time? Does every contemporary work of art have to end with an affirmative? Joyce, with his coda of yesses in *Ulysses*, Beckett, with the "I will go on" of his trilogy, and those 1,001 phallically erected obelisks and church spires pointing optimistically toward the heavens—for once, just once, let a negative prevail.

My conclusion was not a lucky accident. It was a valid, pertinent statement of Debierue's life and art. Skipping two spaces, I put a "—30—" to the piece.

I was suddenly tired. My neck and shoulders were sore and my back ached. I looked at my watch. Six o'clock. There was a plaintive rumble in my hollow stomach. Except for going into the can three times, I had been at the typewriter for almost six straight hours. I got up, stretched, rubbed the back of my neck, and walked around the coffee table shaking my hands and fingers above my head to get rid of the numb feeling in my arms.

I was tired but I wasn't sleepy. I was exhilarated by completing the article in such a short time. Every part had fallen neatly into place, and I knew that it was a good piece of writing. I had never felt better in my entire life.

I sighed, put the cover on the Hermes, moved the typewriter to the bed, and sat at the desk again to read and correct the article. I righted spelling errors, changed some diction, and penciled in a rough transitional sentence between two disparate paragraphs. It wasn't good enough, and I made a note in the margin to rewrite it. One long convoluted sentence with three semicolons and two colons made me laugh aloud. My mind had really been racing on that one. I reduced it, without any trouble, to four clear, separate sentences—

The phone rang, a loud, jangling ring designed to arouse traveling salesmen who had been drinking too much before going to bed. I almost jumped out of my chair.

Berenice's voice was husky. "I'm hungry."

"Who isn't?"

"I've been sleeping."

"I've been working."

"I've been awake for a half hour, but I'm too lazy to get out of bed. Why don't you come over and get in with me?"

"Jesus, Berenice, I've been working all day and I'm tired as hell."

"If you eat something, you'll feel better."

"All right. Give me an hour, and I'll be over."

"Should I order dinner sent up?"

"No. I prefer to eat something hot, and I've never had a hot meal served in a hotel room. We'll go down to the dining room."

"I'll do my nails."

"In an hour." I racked the phone.

I finished reading and proofing the typescript and put the manuscript in a manila envelope before tucking it safely away in my suitcase. There were only minimal changes to be made in New York. Only two pages would require rewriting. I put the canvas, ashtray palette, and other art materials into the closet. I could paint the picture after dinner.

The tub in the bathroom was huge, the old-fashioned kind with big claw feet clutching metal balls. The hot water came boiling out, and I shaved while the tub filled. The water was much too hot to get into, but I added a little cold water at a time until the temperature dropped to the level I could stand. Sliding down into the steaming, man-sized tub until I was fully submerged, except for my face, I soaked up the heat. The soreness gradually left my back and shoulders. I finished with a cold shower, and by the time I was dressed, I felt as if I had had eight hours' sleep. I called the bar, ordered two Gibsons to be sent to 510, Berenice's room, and studied the road maps I had picked up at the last Standard station.

After dinner, I figured I could paint the picture in an hour or at most an hour and a half. Now that the article was finished there was no point in staying overnight at the hotel. I wasn't sleepy, and with both of us driving we could make it to New York in about thirty hours. The front wheels of the old car started to shimmy if I tried to push it beyond fifty-five mph, but thirty hours from Valdosta was a fairly accurate estimate. I had forty dollars in my wallet and some loose change. My Standard credit card would get the car to New York, but I decided to save my cash. Berenice had traveler's checks, and she could use some of them to pay the hotel tab. Through the cracked door, I heard the bellman knock on 510 across the way. I waited until Berenice signed the chit and the waiter had caught the down elevator before I crossed the hallway and knocked on her door.

Berenice was willowy in a blue slack suit with lemon, quarter-inch lines forming windowpane checks, and the four tightly grouped buttons of the double-breasted jacket were genuine lapis lazuli. The bells of the slacks were fully sixteen inches in diameter, and only the toes of her white wedgies were exposed. There was a silk penny-colored scarf around her neck. She had done her nails in Chen Yu nail varnish, that peculiar decadent shade of red that resembles dried blood (the sexiest shade of red ever made, and so Germanic thirtiesish that Visconti made Ingrid Thulin wear it in *The Damned*), and she had painted her lips to match. During her six weeks in Palm Beach, Berenice had learned some peculiar things about fashion, but the schoolteacher from Duluth had not disappeared.

She giggled and pointed to the tray on the coffee table. "These are supposed to be Gibsons!"

There were two miniatures of Gilbey's gin and another of Stock dry vermouth (two tenths of gin, an eighth of vermouth), a glass pitcher with chunks, not cubes, of ice, and a tiny glass bowl containing several cocktail onions.

I shrugged. "I don't think they're allowed to serve mixed drinks in this Georgia county, although the waiter would've mixed them for you if you'd tipped him. Actually"—I twisted the metal caps off the two gin miniatures—"it's better this way. Most bartenders overuse vermouth in Gibsons, and I'd rather make my own anyway."

"It just struck me funny, that's all," Berenice said.

While I mixed the Gibsons, I tried to work out a simple plan and a way of presenting it to Berenice to keep her away from my room until we were ready to leave.

"Did you go to a movie this afternoon?"

She shook her head, and sipped her cocktail. "I wouldn't go to a movie alone back home, much less in a strange town. I'm not the scary type, you know that, James, but there are some things a woman shouldn't do alone, and that's one of them."

"At any rate, you got through the day."

"I slept like the dead. How's the article coming?"

"That's what I wanted to talk to you about. I finished it."

"Already? That's wonderful, James!"

"It's a good rough draft," I admitted, "but it'll need a few things filled in up in New York—"

"Am I in it? Can I read it?"

"No. It's an article about Debierue and his art, not about you and me. When did you become interested in art criticism?" I grinned.

"When I met Mr. Debierue, that's when." She smiled. "He's the nicest, sweetest old gentleman I ever met."

"I'd rather you'd wait till I have the final draft, if you don't mind. I want to get back to New York as soon as possible to finish it. So after dinner, I'll take a short nap until midnight, and then we can check out of here and get rolling. If we trade off on the driving, we can reach the city in about thirty hours."

"You won't get much sleep if we leave at midnight . . ."

"I don't need much, and you've already had enough. You wouldn't be able to sleep much tonight anyway, not after being in the sack all day."

"I'm not arguing, James, I was just worried about you—"

"In that case, let's go downstairs to dinner, so I can come back up and get some sleep before midnight."

During dinner, Berenice asked me if she could see Debierue's picture, but I put her off by telling her it was all wrapped up securely in the trunk of the car, and that it wouldn't be a good idea for anyone to see us looking at a painting in the basement garage. I reminded her conspiratorially that it was a "hot" picture, and we didn't want anyone suspecting us and making inquiries. Because I half-whispered this explanation, she nodded solemnly and accepted it.

The food was excellent—medium-rare sirloins, corn on the cob, okra and tomatoes, creamed scalloped potatoes, a cucumber and onion salad, with a chocolate pudding dessert topped with real whipped cream, not sprayed from a can—and I ate every bit of it, including four hot biscuits with butter (my two, and Berenice's two). I felt somewhat logy following the heavy meal, but after drinking two cups of black coffee, although I was uncomfortably stuffed, I still wasn't sleepy.

I signed the check and penciled in my room number. "After all that food, I'm sleepy," I said.

Berenice took my arm as we left the dining room to cross the lobby to the elevators. "Wouldn't you like a little nightcap," she squeezed my arm, "to make you sleep better—in my room?"

"No," I replied, "and when I say No to an offer like that you know I'm sleepy enough already."

I took her room key, opened the door, and kissed her good night. "I'll leave a call for eleven thirty, and then I'll knock on your door. Try and get some more sleep."

"If I can," she replied, "and if not, I'll watch television. Let me have another one of those good-night kisses . . ."

My room was musty and close again, although I had not turned off the overhead fan. I didn't want to go through the too-hot—too-cold routine with the reverse-cycle air-conditioner—which had far too many BTUs for the size of the small room—so I cracked the door again and clamped it open with the brass hook-and-eye attachment. I stripped down to my shorts and T-shirt, took the art materials out of the closet, and got busy with the picture.

I mixed Prussian blue, adding zinc white a dollop at a time, until I had a color the shade of an Air Force uniform. I thinned it slightly with turpentine and brushed a patch on the bottom of the canvas. It was still too dark, and I added white until the blue became much bolder. I then mixed enough of the diluted blue to paint a slightly ragged border, not less than an inch in width, nor more than three inches, around the four sides of the rectangle. To fill the remaining white space with burnt orange was simple enough, once I was able to get the exact shade I wanted, but it took me much longer than I expected to mix it, because it wasn't easy to match a color that I could see in my mind, but not in front of me.

But the color was rich when I achieved it to my satisfaction. Not quite brown, not quite mustardy, but a kind of burnished burnt orange with a felt, rather than an observable, sense of yellow. I mixed more of the paint than I would need, to be sure that I would have enough, and thinned the glowing pile with enough linseed oil and turpentine to spread it smoothly on the canvas. Using the largest brush, I filled in the center of the canvas almost to the blue border, and then changed to a smaller brush to carefully fill in the narrow ring of white space that remained.

I backed to the wall for a long view of the completed painting, and decided that the blue border was not quite ragged enough. This was remedied in a few minutes, and the painting was as good as my description of it in my article. In fact, the picture was so bright and shining under the floor lamp, it looked even better than I had expected.

All it needed was Debierue's signature.

I had a sharp debate with myself whether to sign it or not, wondering whether it was in keeping with the philosophy of the "American Harvest" period for him to put his name on one of the pictures. But inasmuch as the burnt orange, blue-bordered painting represented the "self" of Debierue, I concluded that if he ever signed a painting, this was one he would *have* to sign. I made a mental note to add this information to my article—that this was the first picture Debierue had ever signed (it would certainly raise the value for Mr. Cassidy to possess a signed painting!).

Debierue's letter to the manager of the French clipping service was still in my jumpsuit. I took it out and studied Debierue's cramped signature, sighing gratefully over the uniqueness of the design. Forgers love a tricky signature: it makes forgery much simpler for them because it is much easier to copy a complicated signature than it is a plain, straightforward signature. There are two ways to forge a signature. One is to practice writing it over and over again until it is perfected. That is the hard way. The easy way is to turn the signature upside down and draw it, not write it, but copy it the way one would imitate any other line drawing. And this is what I did. Actually, I didn't have to turn the canvas upside down. By copying Debierue's signature onto the upper left-hand side upside down, when the picture itself was turned upside down the top would then be the bottom, and the signature would be rightside up and in the lower right-hand corner where it belonged.

Nevertheless, it took me a long time to copy it, because I was trying to paint it as small as possible in keeping with Debierue's practice of writing tiny letters. To put *ebierue* inside the "D" wasn't simple, and I had to remember to "write" with my brushstrokes up instead of down, because that is the way the strokes would have to be when the painting was turned upside down.

"*James!*"

Berenice called out my name. I was so deeply engrossed in what I was doing I wasn't certain whether this was the first or the second time she had called it out. But it was too late to do anything about it. I was sitting in the straight-backed chair facing the canvas, and I barely had time to turn and look at her, much less get to my feet, before she lifted the brass hook, opened the door, and entered the room.

"James," she repeated flatly, halting abruptly with her hand still on the doorknob. She had removed her makeup, and her pale pink lips made a round "O" as she stared at me, the canvas, and the make-shift palette on the low coffee table. The sheet I had used to wrap the once-blank canvas was on the floor and gathered about the chair I was using as an easel. I had spread it there to prevent paint from dropping onto the rug.

"Yes?" I said quietly.

Berenice shut the door, and leaned against it. She supported herself with her hands flat against the door panels. "Just now . . . on TV," she said, not looking at me, but with her rounded blue eyes staring at the canvas, ". . . on the ten thirty news, the newscaster said that Debierue's house had burned down."

"Anything else?"

She nodded. "Pending an investigation—something like that—Mr. Debierue will be the house guest of the famous criminal lawyer Joseph Cassidy in Palm Beach."

I swallowed, and nodded my head. I am a highly verbal individual, but for once in my life I was at a loss for words. One lie after another struggled for expression in my mind, but each lie, in turn, was rejected before it could be voiced.

"Is that Debierue's painting?" Berenice said, as she crossed the room toward my chair.

"Yes. I needed to look at it again, you see, to check it against the description in my article. It was slightly damaged—Debierue's signature—so I thought I'd touch it up some."

Berenice pressed her forefinger to the exact center of the painting. She examined the wet, bemerded smear on her fingertip.

"Oh, James," she said unhappily, "you painted this awful picture . . . !"

3

LOOKING BACK (and faced with the same set of circumstances), I don't know that I would have handled the problem any differently—except for some minor changes from the way that I did solve it. Ignorant women have destroyed the careers, the ambitions, and the secret plans of a good many honorable men throughout history.

It would have been easy enough to blame myself for allowing Berenice to discover the painting. If I had locked the door, instead of being concerned with my physical discomfort in the hotel room, I could have hidden the painting from her before allowing her into the room. This one little slip on my part destroyed everything, if one wants to look at it that way. But the problem was greater than this—not a matter of just one little slip. There was an entire string of unfortunate coincidences, going back to the unwitting moment I had allowed Berenice to move in on me, and continuing through my foolhardy decision to allow her to accompany me to Debierue's house.

And now, of course, caught red handed—or burnt orange handed—Berenice was in possession of a lifelong hold over me if I carried my deception through—with the publication of the article, with the sending of the painting to Joseph Cassidy, to say nothing of the future, *my* future, and the subsequent furor that the publication of an article on Debierue would arouse in the art world.

Berenice loved me, or so she had declared again and again, and if I had married her, perhaps she would have kept her mouth shut, carrying her secret knowledge, and mine, to her grave. I don't know. I doubted it then, and I doubt it now. Love, according to my experience, is a fragile transitory emotion. Not only does love fall a good many years short of lasting forever, a long stretch for love to last is a few months, or even a few weeks. If I think about my friends and acquaintances in New York—and don't consider casual acquaintances I have known elsewhere, in Palm Beach, for example—I can't think of a single friend, male or female, who hasn't been divorced at least once. And most of them, *more* than once. The milieu I live in is that way. The art world is not only egocentric, it is egoeccentric. The environment is not conducive to lasting friendships, let alone lasting marriages. And that was my world . . .

My remaining choice, which was too stupid even to consider seriously, was a bitter one. I could have destroyed *The Burnt Orange Heresy* (such was the title I assigned to the painting), and torn up the article I had written, which would mean that the greatest opportunity I had ever had to make a name for myself as an art critic would be lost.

These thoughts were jumbled together in my mind as I confronted Berenice, but not in any particular order. Emotionally, I was only mildly annoyed at the time, knowing I had a major problem to solve, but bereft, at least for the moment, of any solution.

"You may believe that this is an 'awful' picture," I said coldly to Berenice, "and it's your privilege to think so if, and the key word is *if*, if you can substantiate your opinion with valid reasons as to *why* it's an 'awful' picture. Otherwise, you're not entitled to any value judgments concerning Debierue's work."

"I—I just can't believe it!" Berenice said, shaking her head. "You're not going to try to pass this off as a painting by Debierue, are you?"

"It *is* a painting by Debierue. Didn't I just tell you that I was touching it up a little because it was damaged slightly in transit?"

"I'm not *blind,* James." She made a helpless, fluttering gesture with her hands, her big eyes taking in the evidence of the art materials and the painting itself. "How do you expect to get away with something so *raw*? Don't you know that Mr. Cassidy will *show* this painting to Debierue, and that—"

"Berenice!" I brought her up sharply. "You're sticking your middle-western nose into something that is none of your damned business! Now get the hell out of here, get packed, and if you aren't ready to leave in twenty minutes, you can damned well stay here in Valdosta!"

Her face flushed, and she took two steps backward. She nodded, nibbled her nether lip, and nodded again. "All *right!* There is obviously something going on that I don't understand, but that isn't any reason to blow off at me like that. You can at least explain it to me. You can't blame me for being bewildered, can you? I can see that, well, the way it looks is *funny,* that's all!"

I got up from the chair, put my arm around her shoulders, and gave her a friendly hug. "I'm sorry," I said gently, "I shouldn't have woofed at you like that. And don't worry. I'll explain everything to you in the car. There's a good girl. Just get packed, and we can get out of here and be on our way in a few minutes. Okay?"

I held open the door. Still nodding her head, Berenice crossed the hallway to her room.

The moment her door closed, I wrapped the art materials in the sheet, washed the ashtray palette under the bathtub hot water tap and dried it with a towel. I slipped on my trousers and a shirt, and took the painting and the small bundle of art materials down to the basement garage on the elevator. I dumped the bundle in a garbage can, and placed the painting carefully, wet side up, in the trunk of my car. It took another three minutes to unfasten the canvas covertible top, fold it back, and snap the fasteners of the plastic cover. It would be chilly riding with the top back at this time of night, but I could put it up again later. The night garage attendant, a young black man wearing white overalls, stood in the doorway of the small, lighted office, watching me silently as I struggled with the top. Finished, I crossed the garage, handed him a quarter, and told him I was checking out.

"Call the desk, please," I said, "and tell the clerk to send a bellman with a truck to get our baggage in five-ten and five-oh-five in about fifteen minutes. Tell the bellman to pile it on the back seat when he comes down. The trunk is already filled with other things."

"Yes, sir," he said.

I returned to my room, packed in less than five minutes, pulled a sleeveless sweater on over my shirt, and slipped into my sports coat. Berenice wasn't ready yet, but I helped her close her suitcases, and advised her to wear her warm polo coat over her slack suit. The bellman came with his truck, and when we got off at the lobby to check out, he continued on down to the basement to put our luggage in the car. Berenice paid the bill, which was surprisingly reasonable, by cashing two traveler's checks, and the bellman had the car out in front for us before we had finished checking out. The night deskman didn't ask questions about why we were leaving in the middle of the night, and I didn't volunteer any information.

The night air was chilly when we got into the car, and there was a light, misty fog hovering fifty feet or so above the deserted city streets. I lit two cigarettes, handed Berenice one of them, and pulled away from the curb. She shivered slightly and huddled down in her seat.

"You're probably wondering why I put the top back," I said.

"Yes, I am. But after the way you barked at me last time, I'm almost afraid to ask any questions."

I laughed and patted her leg. "If it gets too cold, I'll put it up again. But I thought it would be best to get as much fresh air as possible to keep myself awake. It isn't really cold, and there won't be much traffic this time of night, so we should make fairly good time."

Berenice accepted this moronic explanation, and I increased the speed the moment we got out of the downtown area and onto the new four-lane highway that was still bordered by residential streets containing two- and three-story houses.

From my examination of the map I knew that there were several small lakes between Valdosta and Tifton, and a few pine reserves as well, first- and second-growth forests to feed the Augusta paper mills. Most of the rich, red land was cultivated, however—tobacco, for the major crop, but also with melons, corn, peas, or anything else that a farmer wanted to grow, including flax. East of Valdosta was the Great Okefenokee Swamp, which filled a large section of southeast Georgia, and there were many small lakes, streams, and brooks that filtered well-silted water into the swamp.

I was unfamiliar with the highway and the countryside, and I didn't know precisely what I was looking for, other than a grove of pines, a finger of swamp, and a rarely used access road. I slowed down considerably a few miles north of Valdosta, as soon as I was in open country with only widely scattered farmhouses, and I began to keep my eyes open for side roads leading nowhere. Berenice, who had been as silent as a martyr, and suffering from my silence as well, finally had to open her mouth.

"Well?" she said.

"Well, what?"

"I'm waiting for the explanation, that's what. You said you'd explain, what are you waiting for?"

"I've been thinking things over, Berenice, and I'm beginning to come to my senses. You really don't think it would be a good idea, do you, to send that painting to Mr. Cassidy?"

"That's your business, James. It isn't up to me to tell you what to do, but if you're asking me for an opinion I'd say no. But as you said, I don't know all there is to know about what it is you're trying to do—so until I do, I'll keep my long 'middle-western nose' out of your business."

"I apologized for that, sweetheart."

"That's all right. I know that my nose fits my face. What does bother me though is that I've been more or less forced to think that you set fire to Debierue's house."

"Me?" I laughed. "What makes you think I'd do something like that?"

"Well, for one thing, you didn't show any surprise," she said shrewdly, "when I told you about the news of the fire on television."

"Why should I be surprised? His villa in France burned down, too. It does surprise me, however, that you would think that I did it."

"Then tell me that you didn't do it, and I'll believe you."

"What would my motive be for doing such a thing?"

"Why not give me a simple yes or no?"

"There are no simple yes or no answers in this world, Big Girl—none that I've ever found. There are only qualified yes and no answers, and not many of them."

"All right, James, I can't think of a valid motive, to use one of your favorite words, 'valid,' but I can think of a motive that *you* might consider valid. I think you've faked an article about some paintings that Debierue was supposed to paint, but didn't paint. You looked at the paintings he did paint and didn't like them, probably because they didn't meet your high standards of what you thought they should be, so you burned them by setting fire to the house. You then invented some nonexistent paintings of your own and wrote about them instead."

"Jesus, do you realize how crazy that sounds?"

"Yes, I do. But you can show me how crazy it is by letting me read the article you wrote. If there's no mention of that weird orange—"

"Burnt orange—"

"All right, *burnt* orange painting in your article, then you can easily prove me wrong. I'll apologize, and that'll be that."

"That'll be *that,* just like that? And then you'll expect me to forgive your wild accusation as if you'd never made it, right?"

"I said that I might be wrong, and I sincerely hope that I am. It's easy enough to prove me wrong, isn't it? What I *do* know though, and there's nothing you can ever say to persuade me that I'm wrong, is that Debierue never painted that picture in your hotel room. *You* painted it. It was still wet when I touched it—including Debierue's signature. And the only reason I can possibly come up with for you to do such a thing is because you want to write about it, and pass it off as Debierue's work. I—I don't know what to think, James, the whole thing has given me a headache. And really—you may not believe this—I actually don't care! *Honestly,* I don't! But I don't want you to get into any trouble, either. Arson is a very serious offense, James."

"No shit?"

"It isn't funny, I'll tell you that much. And if you did set fire to Debierue's house, you should tell me!"

"Why? So you can turn me in to the police for arson?"

"Oh, James," she wailed. Berenice put her face into cupped hands and began to cry.

"All right, Berenice," I said quietly, after I had let her cry for a minute or so, "I'll tell you what I'm going to do." I handed her my handkerchief.

She shook her head, took a Kleenex tissue out of her purse, and blew her nose with a refined honk.

"You're right, Berenice, on all counts," I continued, "and I might as well admit it. I guess I got carried away, but it isn't too late. Setting the fire was an accident. I didn't do it on purpose. The old man had spilled some turpentine, and I accidentally dropped my cigarette and it caught. I thought I'd put it out, but apparently it flared up again. Do you see?"

She nodded. "I thought it was something like that."

"That's the way it happened, I guess. But painting the picture was another matter. I don't know how I expected to get away with it, and the chances are I would've chickened out at the last minute anyway. What I'll do is throw the picture away, and then rewrite the article altogether, using the information I've actually got."

"He told us lots of interesting things."

"Sure he did."

There was a dirt road on the right, leading into a thick stand of pines. I made the turn, shifted down to second gear, but kept up the engine speed because of the sand.

"Where are you going?"

"I'm going to drive back in here well off the highway and burn the painting."

"You can wait until morning, can't you?"

"No. I think that the sooner I get rid of it the better. If I kept it I might change my mind again. It *would* be possible, you know, to get away with it—"

"No, it wouldn't, James," she said crisply.

The sandy road, after more than a mile, ended in a small clearing. The clearing was filled with knee-high grass, and we were completely surrounded by second-growth slash pine. It would be another two years, at least, before these trees would be tall enough to cut. I left the lights on and cut the engine. Without another word I got out of the car, opened the trunk with the key, and picked up the tire iron. It was about ten inches long, quite hefty, and the flattened end, although it wasn't sharp, was thin enough to make a good cutting edge. Rounding the car on Berenice's side, I brought the heavy iron down on her head.

"Ooauh!" She expelled her breath, clasped both hands over her head, and turned her face toward me. Her eyes were wide and staring, but her face was expressionless. I hadn't hit her hard enough, or I had miscalculated the thickness of her hair, piled on top of her head, which had cushioned the blow. I hit her on top of the head again, much harder this time, and she slumped down in the seat.

I opened the door, grabbed the thick collar of her polo coat, and dragged her out of the car. She was inert, unbelievably heavy, and her left leg was still in the front seat. I was working one-handed, still clutching the tire iron in my right hand, and trying to free her leg from the car door, when she convulsed, rolled over, and came up off the ground, head down, butting me in the stomach like a goat.

Caught by surprise, I fell backward and my shoulder hit a splintered tree stump. At the same time my left elbow banged against the ground sharply, right on the ulna bone. My right shoulder felt as if it were on fire, and crazy prickles from my banged funny bone danced inside my forearm. I dropped the tire iron, rubbed my right shoulder with the fingers of my left hand, and the pain in my elbow and shoulder gradually subsided. Through the trees, and getting farther away every second, Berenice's voice screamed shrilly. I picked up the tire iron.

I turned off the headlights and started after her, judging direction by the sound of her screams, which were growing fainter, in the dark forest. Berenice ran awkwardly, like most women, and she was hampered by the knee-length coat. I didn't think she could run far, but I was unable to catch up with her. I tried to run myself, but after tripping over a stump and sprawling full length on the damp ground, I settled for a fast walk.

The screaming stopped, and so did I. The abrupt silence startled me and, for the first time, I was frightened. I had to find her. If she got away, everything was over for me—everything.

I moved ahead, walking slower now, searching every foot of ground, now that my eyes had become adjusted to the dim light. A light mist hovered a hundred feet above the trees, but there was a moon, and I could see a little better with every passing moment. The trees thinned out and the wet ground began to get mushy. I was on the edge of a swamp, and after another fifty yards or so, I came to the edge of a lake of black, stagnant water. I knew Berenice well enough to know that she wouldn't have plunged into that inky water. The way was easier going toward the left, and I took it, figuring that she would do the same.

I found her a few minutes later, catching sight of her light-colored coat. She was in a prone position, with her legs spread awkwardly, partially hidden under a spreading dogwood tree. Afraid to touch her, I rolled her over on her back. A pale shaft of moonlight filtered through the tree branches, lighting her bloody face and wide staring eyes.

I didn't know whether she was dead or not, but I had to make certain. There was one thing I did know. I wouldn't have been able to hit her again. As I knelt down beside her and opened her coat, an aroma of Patou's Joy filled my nostrils with loss. I put my head down on her chest and listened for a heartbeat. Nothing. Berenice was dead, but my blows on her head hadn't killed her. She had died from shock. No one, mortally wounded, would have been able to run so far. On the other hand, both of us for a few moments had been gifted with superhuman strength. She was a big woman, stronger than hell, and she had been fighting for her life.

But so had I.

I dragged her to the edge of the water and wedged her body under a fallen tree that was half in and half out of the swamp. By leaning dead branches and by piling brush over the unsubmerged part of the tree, she was completely hidden from view. Debierue knew that she was with me, and if she were to be found, and if he learned that she had been killed, he would tell Cassidy immediately. That is, he would tell Cassidy if her body was found before he received the tear sheets of my article on his American Harvest period. He would be so delighted by my article he wouldn't risk mentioning Berenice's name to anyone. His reputation, as well as mine, depended upon that article. But there would be time, plenty of time. Months, perhaps years, would pass before her body was found.

Suddenly I was weak and dispirited. All of my strength disappeared. I leaned against the nearest tree and vomited my dinner—the corn, the tomatoes and okra, the stringy chunks of sirloin, the biscuits, everything. Panting and sobbing until I caught my breath, I returned to the dogwood tree and picked up my tire iron. It had my fingerprints on it, and in case I had a flat tire on my way to New York, I would need it again.

I started back toward the car, and after walking for five minutes or so I discovered that I was lost. I panicked and began to run. I tripped and fell, banging my head against a tree, scratching a painful gash in my forehead. As Freud said, there are no accidents. Fighting down my panic by taking long deep breaths, I calmed down further by forcing myself to sit quietly on the damp ground, with my back against a tree, and by smoking a cigarette down to the cork tip. I was all right. Everything was going to be all right.

Calmer now, although my hands were still trembling, I managed to retrace my path back to the swamp and Berenice. I now had a sense of direction. I started back in what I thought was the general direction of the car, and hit the sandy road, missing the clearing and the car by about fifty yards. My face was flushed with heat, and I was shivering at the same time with cold. Before setting out, I put up the canvas top, and then kicked over the engine.

Two weeks later, back in New York, when I was cleaning out the car in order to sell it, I found one of Berenice's fingers, or a part of one—the first two joints and the Chen Yu-ed fingernail. She must have got it lopped off when she had put her hands over her head in the car. I wrapped the finger in a handkerchief and put it safely away. Perhaps a day would come, I thought, when I would be able to look at this finger without fear, pain, or remorse.

4

THE PHOTOGRAPH OF Debierue "reading" the flaming copy of the *Miami Herald,* which illustrated my article in *Fine Arts: The Americas* was republished in *Look* and *Newsweek,* and in the fine arts section of the *Sunday New York Times.* UPI, after dickering with my agent, finally bought the photo and sent it out on the wire to their subscribers. The money I made from this photo provided me with my first tailor-made suit. Coat and trousers, four hundred dollars.

I had made one side trip off the superhighway to Baltimore, on my way back to New York, where I checked Berenice's luggage in two lockers inside the Greyhound bus station (including her handbag and traveler's checks, knowing that her mother could use this money someday, if and when the bags were ever claimed). Except for this brief stopover, I drove straight through to the city.

There were five message slips in my office telling me to telephone Joseph Cassidy, collect, immediately, so I called him before I did anything else.

"Did you get the picture?" he asked.

"Yes, of course."

"Good! Good! Hold it for a few days before sending it down. I want to get Mr. Debierue settled in a good nursing home, you see—he doesn't know that you have the painting, does he?"

"No, and it'll be better if he doesn't. I've mentioned it in my article, although I won't run a photograph of it. Before sending it to Palm Beach I intend to take some good color plates of *The Burnt Orange Heresy* for *eventual* publication, if you get what I mean . . ."

"Naturally—is that the title, *The Burnt Orange Heresy*? That's great!"

"Yeah. It'll probably have an additional title, too. *Self-portrait.*"

"Jesus—James, I can hardly wait to see it!"

"Just let me know when, Mr. Cassidy, and I'll send it down to you air express."

"Don't worry, I'll call you. And listen, James, I'm not going to forget this. When the time comes to exhibit it, you've got an exclusive to cover the opening."

"Thanks."

"My problem right now is to persuade Debierue to enter a rest home. He's much too old to take care of himself. If he had been asleep when the fire started, he would've been killed you know. And when I think of those paintings that went up in smoke—Jesus!"

"Did he tell you anything about them?"

"Not a word. You know how he is. And nothing seems to faze him. He spends most of his time just sitting around watching old movies on TV and drinking orange juice. He can do that in a rest home. Well, you'll hear from me. This is a long distance call, you know."

"Sure. Later."

He didn't call me again, however. He sent me a special delivery letter after he had settled Debierue in the Regal Pines Nursing Home, near Melbourne, Florida. I sent Cassidy the painting, air express collect, although I had to pay the insurance fee, in advance, before they would agree to send it collect.

The critical reaction to my article, when it appeared in *Fine Arts: The Americas,* followed the pattern I had anticipated. Canaday, in the

Times, had reservations. Perreault, in *The Village Voice,* was enthusiastic, and there was a short two-paragraph item in *The L.A. Free Press* recommending the article to would-be revolutionary painters in Southern California. This was more newspaper coverage than I expected.

My real concern was with the concentric ripples in the art journals and critical quarterlies. This reaction was slow in coming, because a lot of thought had to be put into them. The best single article, which set off a long string of letters in the correspondence department, appeared in *Spectre,* and was written by Pierre Montrand. A French chauvinist, he saw Debierue's "American Harvest" period as a socialistic rejection of DeGaullism. This was an absurd idea, but beautifully expressed, and controversial as hell.

With my photograph of Debierue, many newspapers printed sketchy accounts of Debierue's mysterious immigration to the United States, but I kept my promise to Cassidy and the old man. I never divulged Debierue's Florida address after Cassidy had him admitted under a false name to the Regal Pines Nursing Home, and Cassidy had covered his tracks so well the reporters never found him. I mailed Debierue the tearsheets of my article, a dozen 8" x 10" photographs of the burning newspaper shot, and an autographed copy of my book, *Art and the Preschool Child.* He didn't acknowledge the package, but I knew that he received it because I had mailed it Return Receipt Requested.

For the first week after my return to New York I bought a daily copy of the *Atlanta Journal-Constitution* (it "covers Dixie like the dew"), and searched through the pages to see if there was any mention of a body being found near Valdosta. But I disliked the newspaper, and searching for such news every day was making me morbid. I quit buying the paper. If they found her, they found her, and there was nothing I could do about it. Inevitably, though, a reaction appeared in my psyche, caused, naturally enough, by the death of Berenice. It wasn't that my conscience bothered me, although that was a part of my reaction. It was a second-thought overlap of self-doubt, a feeling of ambivalence that vitiated my value judgments of the new work I witnessed. I overcame this feeling, or overreaction, by compartmentalizing Debierue in a corner of my mind. I was able to rid myself of my ambivalence by setting Debierue apart from other artists as a "one-of-a-kind" painter, and by not considering him in connection with the mainstream of contemporary art. It didn't take too many weeks before I adjusted to this mental suggestion. I was able to function normally again on my regular critical assignments.

My reputation as a critic didn't soar, but my workload doubled and, with it, my income. Tom Russell gave me a fifty-dollar raise, which brought me up to four fifty a month at the magazine. My lecture fee was raised, and I gave more lectures, including a lecture at Columbia on "New Trends in Contemporary Art" to the art majors—and the Fine Arts Department paid me a six-hundred-dollar lecture fee. To lecture in my old school, where I had once been a poverty-stricken graduate student, was perhaps the high point of the entire year.

My agent unloaded some older, unsold articles I had written months before—two of them to art magazines which had earlier rejected them.

I had always done a certain amount of jury work, judging art shows for "expenses only," and more often without any compensation at all. I now began to receive some decent cash offers to judge and hang important exhibits at major museums. On a jury show I served on at Hartford, there was a Herb Westcott painting entered in the show. Westcott had changed his style to Romantic Realism, and his fine, almost delicate draftsmanship was well suited to the new style. The Hartford show had an antipollution theme, and Westcott had painted an enormous blowup of a 1925 postcard view of Niagara

Falls. The painting wasn't in the First Prize category, but I was able to persuade the other jury members (the museum director and Maury Katz, a hard-edge painter) to tag Westcott's painting with an honorable mention and a thousand-dollar purchase prize. I had treated Westcott rather shabbily in Palm Beach, running out on him and his show at Gloria's Gallery, and it pleased me to give him a leg up—which he well deserved in any case.

Now included in my books to review were books that the managing editor used to reserve for himself—beautiful, expensive, handsomely illustrated, coffee-table art books—that retailed for twenty-five, thirty-five, and even fifty dollars. After being reviewed, these expensive books can be sold at half of their wholesale price to bookdealers. This pocketed cash is found money I.R.S. investigators cannot discover easily.

I no longer slept well. I didn't sleep well at all.

I knew that Debierue had read my article, and although I had made an educated guess that he would say nothing, I could not be positive that he would continue to say nothing. I had dared to assume that four important European art critics had also invented imaginary paintings by Debierue to write about. But *they* couldn't denounce me. Only Debierue could do that and, thanks to the fire I had set, he couldn't actually prove anything.

Nevertheless, late at night, I often awoke from a fitful sleep, covered with perspiration. Sitting in the dark on the edge of my bed, trying to keep my mind as blank as possible, I would light one cigarette after another, afraid to go back to sleep. In time, I would tell myself, all in good time, my nightmares would run their course and stop.

A year later, almost to the day that I returned to New York, Debierue died in Florida. Mr. Cassidy wired me, inviting me to the funeral, but I was tied up with other work and couldn't get away on such short notice. Bodies, in Florida, must be buried within twenty-four hours, according to the state law. I wrote the obituary—a black-bordered one-page tribute—for the magazine, of course, inasmuch as I was *the* authority on Debierue, and had already written the definitive piece on him for the forthcoming *International Encyclopedia of Fine Arts.*

Ten days after Debierue's death I received a long, bulky package at the office. When I unwrapped it at my desk I discovered the dismantled baroque frame that had once been Debierue's famous *No. One.* This unexpected gift from beyond the grave made me cry, the first time I had wept in several months. There was no personal note or card with the frame. Debierue had probably left word with someone at the nursing home to mail it to me after he died. But the fact that he sent me the frame meant exoneration. Not only a complete exoneration, it proved that he had been pleased by my critique of his "American Harvest" period. From all of his many critics, Debierue had singled me out as his beneficiary for *No. One.*

The dismantled frame had no intrinsic value, of course. I probably could have sold it somewhere, or donated it to the Museum of Modern Art for its curiosity value, but I couldn't do that to the old man. His gesture deeply moved me.

I walked down the hall to throw the frame down the incinerator. As I opened the metal door, I noticed a small dead fly scotch-taped to one of the sides of the frame. The old man, despite his age, had a keen memory. After seeing the fly, I couldn't throw the parts down the chute. On my way home from the office I left the bundled frame under my seat in the subway instead.

I had some correspondence with Joseph Cassidy concerning *The Burnt Orange Heresy.* He wanted me to suggest the best place for unveiling it for the public, New York or Chicago. I advised him to wait and to exhibit the painting at Palm Beach instead, at the opening of the next season, to coincide, as nearly as possible, with the publication date of the *International Encyclopedia of Fine Arts,* which would have a full-page color plate of the painting facing my definitive article on the painter . . .

. . . I OPENED THE heavy volume and found my piece on Jacques Debierue. The color plate of *The Burnt Orange Heresy* was a beautiful reproduction of the painting. Reduced in size, color photographs often look better than the original oils. And this colored photo, on expensive, white-coated stock, shone like burnished gold.

I read my article carefully. There were no errors in spelling, and no typographical errors. My name was spelled correctly at the end of the article. A short bibliography of the books and major critical articles on Debierue followed my by-line, set in 5½-point agate boldface. There were no typos in the bibliography, either.

Satisfied, I began to leaf through some of the other volumes of the Encyclopedia, here and there, to check the writing and the quality of the work. I read pieces on some of my favorites—Goya, El Greco, Piranesi, Michelangelo.

My stomach became queasy, and I had a peculiar premonition. The articles I had read were well researched and well written, particularly the piece on Piranesi, but my stomach felt as if it had been filled with raw bread dough that was beginning to rise and swell inside me. I opened my desk drawer and took out my brass ruler. Taking my time, to make certain there would be no mistakes, I measured the column inches in the *Encyclopedia* to see how many inches had been allotted to Goya, El Greco, Piranesi, Michelangelo—and Debierue.

Goya had nine and one-half inches. El Greco had twelve. Piranesi had eight. Michelangelo had fourteen. But Debierue had *sixteen column inches!* The old man, insofar as *space* was concerned, had topped the greatest artists of all time.

I closed the books, all of them, and returned them to the crate. I lit a cigarette and moved to the window. The buttery sunlight of Palm Beach scattered gold coins beneath the poinciana tree outside my window. The dark green grass in the apartment-house courtyard was still wet from the sprinklers the yardman had recently turned off. The pale blue sky, without any clouds, unpolluted by industrial smoke, was as clear as expensively bottled water. I wasn't fooled by the air-conditioning of the room. It was hotter than hell outside in the sun.

But my work was over. Debierue had triumphed over everyone, and so had I. There would never be another Jacques Debierue, not in my lifetime, and I would never want to meet another one like him if one ever did come along. There was no place else for me to go as an art critic. How could I top myself? Not in *this* world.

But what about Berenice Hollis? Could I pass the test? In a cigar box in the bottom drawer of my dresser, together with a picture of my father, taken when he was seven years old, and a dry, rough periwinkle shell (a reminder, because I had picked it up on the beach as a kid, that I was born in Puerto Rico), was Berenice's dried finger, wrapped in a linen handkerchief. I unrolled the handkerchief and looked at the shriveled finger. The blood-red Chen Yu nail varnish was dull, and some of it had flaked off. I looked at the finger for a long time without feeling fear, pain, or remorse.

Debierue, and his achievement, had been worth it, and there was nothing else left for me to do. Somebody else, another critic, could cover the unveiling of Cassidy's only signed Debierue at the Everglades Club. The time had come for me to pay my dues for the death of Berenice Hollis.

I showered, shaved, and put on my tailor-made suit, together with a white shirt, a wide red-white-and-blue striped tie, black silk socks, and polished cordovan shoes.

Taking my time, strolling, I walked through the late afternoon streets to the Spanish-style Palm Beach police station. No one else would ever know the truth about Debierue, and no one, other than myself, knew the truth about my part in his apotheosis. And I would never tell, never, but I had to pay for Berenice. The man who achieves success in America must pay for it. It's the American way, and no one knows this fact of life any better than I, a de–islanded Puerto Rican.

There were a sergeant and two patrolmen inside the station. One patrolman was going on duty and the other was going off, but they both looked so clean and well groomed it would have been impossible to tell them apart. All three policemen were looking at a copy of *Palm Beach Life,* the slick, seasonal magazine that covers Palm Beach society. The policeman going off duty had his picture in it—a shot of a group of women on a garden tour, and he was smiling in the background.

"Good afternoon, sir," the sergeant said politely, getting to his feet, "may I help you?"

I nodded. "Good afternoon, Sergeant," I replied. I unfolded the handkerchief on the table, and Berenice's finger rolled out. "I want to confess to a crime of passion."

About the Author

CHARLES WILLEFORD was a professional horse trainer, boxer, radio announcer, and painter, as well as the author of over a dozen novels, including *The Burnt Orange Heresy, Pick-Up, Cockfighter,* and *Miami Blues,* a collection of short stories, and a memoir of his war experiences. He was a tank commander with the Third Army in World War II. For his war efforts he received the Silver Star, the Bronze Star, the Purple Heart, and the Luxembourg Croix de Guerre. He also studied art in Biarritz, France, and in Lima, Peru, and English at the University of Miami. He died in 1988.